The Manny Files

The
Manny
Files

★ Christian Burch ★

Atheneum Books for Young Readers
New York ★ London ★ Toronto ★ Sydney

Atheneum Books for Young Readers ★ An imprint of Simon & Schuster Children's Publishing Division ★ 1230 Avenue of the Americas ★ New York, New York 10020 ★ This book is a work of fiction. Any references to historical events, real people, or real locales are used fictitiously. Other names, characters, places, and incidents are products of the author's imagination, and any resemblance to actual events or locales or persons, living or dead, is entirely coincidental. ★ Copyright © 2006 by Christian Burch ★ All rights reserved, including the right of reproduction in whole or in part in any form. ★ Book design by Kristin Smith and Jessica Sonkin ★ The text for this book is set in Egyptian 505 BT Roman. ★ Manufactured in the United States of America ★ First Edition ★ 10 9 8 7 6 5 4 3 2 1 ★ Library of Congress Cataloging-in-Publication Data ★ Burch, Christian. ★ The Manny Files / Christian Burch.—1st ed. ★ p.   cm. ★ Summary: A shy young boy learns how to be more outgoing and self-confident from his male nanny. ★ ISBN-13: 978-1-4169-0039-9 ★ ISBN-10: 1-4169-0039-X ★ [1. Nannies—Fiction. 2. Sex role—Fiction. 3. Self-confidence—Fiction. 4. Family life—Fiction. ★ 5. Brothers and sisters—Fiction.] I. Title. ★ PZ7.B91583Ma 2006 ★ [Fic]—dc22   2004026957

To Mom, Dad, and Amy
with love

And to
Scotty and Sage Craighead;
Laramie, India, Keats, and Marrakech Maxwell;
Henley Blayne Turner;
and Fletcher Christian Whittington—
Thank you for sharing your childhoods with me.

★ ACKNOWLEDGMENTS ★

Thank you to Alexandra Fuller and Caitlyn Dlouhy
for helping me bring this farther
than I could have done alone.

. . . And Wished I Were an Only Child

You probably won't remember it later, but my name is Keats. I'm the smallest boy in my class. Actually, it's worse than that. I'm the smallest *person* in my grade. My third-grade teacher never calls on me for answers because she can't see me. I sit behind a tall girl with red poofy hair.

I wish I had red poofy hair.

My hair is the same color as dead grass in November.

My teacher is named Ms. Grant. Ms. Grant is from the South and says things like "y'all" and "fixin' to." My older sister Lulu was in her class a few years ago. Whenever we have to write a book report or do an art project, Ms. Grant shows us one of Lulu's old assignments as an example. When we made snowflakes to hang from the ceiling, she pulled one out from her closet that was covered in colorful sequins and battery-operated Christmas lights. Ms. Grant said, "Y'all, this was made by Keats's older sister," as she pointed to Lulu's school picture on her bulletin board.

The girl with the red poofy hair raised her hand and asked, "Who's Keats?"

I wasn't looking where I was cutting and cut myself with the scissors.

I had to go to the school nurse to get a Big Bird Band-Aid.

Lulu is president of the seventh-grade class. Mom calls her an overachiever. Lulu hates the sound of some words, like *saliva*. I made her cry once by writing the words *panty hose* on her math homework. One Halloween she used mascara to paint her eyebrows together, and put on a colorful dress that Mom bought for her in Mexico. She made a heart out of clay and carried it around. She said that she was Frida Kahlo, the tragic Mexican painter. I dressed up as a television news anchor. Instead of saying "Trick or treat," I said, "Our top story tonight: Children across America dress up in elaborate costumes in hopes of receiving handfuls of treats. More on this story after you give me some candy." Nobody knew what I was supposed to be.

My other older sister, India, usually dresses up as a butterfly for Halloween. In fact, most of the time she looks like a butterfly. She wears bright, rainbow-striped tights and flashy hair bows. She's the only girl at our school who carries a purse instead of a backpack. At the last parent-teacher conference her fourth-grade teacher told Mom and Dad that when she had asked India what she wanted to be when she grew up, India's response was, "I'm just going to get by on my looks." Dad laughed and Mom kicked him underneath the table. Dad thinks that India is going to be a brilliant clothing designer someday.

Dad says the word *brilliant* a lot.

India has a sign on her bedroom door that says, DO NOT ENTER. THIS MEANS YOU, BELLY. Belly is my three-year-old baby sister, whose real name is Mirabelle. We call her Belly because she hates to wear clothes. One time my mom took Belly and me to the mall to buy me the bow tie that I wanted for my birthday. It was silk with yellow and blue stripes and looked exactly like the one that I had circled in the catalog. When we were inside the mall, Belly screamed with glee and ran to the fountain that was filled with glittering pennies on the bottom. I used to scream and run to the fountain when I was littler, but now I just racewalk. My mom dug through her purse for a penny so that I could toss it in and make a secret wish. While Mom was struggling to find a penny, Belly stripped naked and, before we could stop her, was stealing other people's wishes from the

3

middle of the fountain. The grandmothers who were walking laps around the mall pointed and laughed at my sister's bare bottom bobbing up and down as she looked for pennies.

Mom grabbed Belly from the fountain and said, "You're crazy," like what she had done was cute.

I threw my penny in the fountain and wished I were an only child.

My dad does business. It looks like fun because he gets to wear a suit and read the *New York Times*. Mom picks out his clothes for work, but I get to pick the tie. Dad says that he always gets compliments on his ties because I have brilliant taste.

Grandma thinks I have brilliant taste too, except she says that I have a "good eye." One time when we visited Grandma's house, I took her a picture that I had painted for her in school. It was an orange and red striped box with a person standing next to it. When I gave it to her, she said, "Oh my, I completely get this piece. It's about getting outside of the box. I love it. What do you call it?"

"Outside of the Box," I said, even though I hadn't really named it. I thought Grandma's interpretation was much better than the real reason why I had painted it (boxes and people are easy to paint).

"Masterpiece," said Grandma.

She didn't hang it on the refrigerator with the rest of the grandchildren gallery. Instead she made me sign and date it, and she put it in a frame. She hung it in her living room right next to a painting that Mom did when she was little. Grandma says that I inherited my artistic ability from my mom. She also says I got my mom's big forehead.

Mom says that a big forehead means you have a big brain. She uses her big brain at the museum downtown where she's a curator. She's in charge of hanging artwork for shows. Whenever I go with her to work, I get to bring home a postcard or coloring book from the museum shop. One time I brought home a post-card with a Picasso painting on it. Picasso paints like I do, with noses and eyes all over the place.

My mom and dad are very smart and very busy, so we have a nanny who helps us.

We have had a lot of nannies.

Our first nanny was named Mary. Mary loved my sisters. When they were little, she used to dress them up in bright, frilly dresses. Mom thought they looked pretty, but Dad said that they looked like piñatas.

"Did it make you want to hit them with sticks?" I asked.

Dad giggled when I said this.

Mary gave Lulu and India hairdos and painted their fingernails and toenails. She gave them necklaces and bracelets with fancy diamonds and jewels hanging from them.

She gave *me* dental floss.

A few years ago Mary got married and had a baby. She sent Mom a picture of the baby. She was bald and looked like a boy except she had a pink bow Scotch-taped to her head.

Then there was Madge. Madge was as old as Grandpa Dub, my dad's dad. Grandpa Dub came over to visit us a lot more when Madge was there. Once when my sisters were gone to piano lessons, he told me that Madge was a tall glass of water and that he was thirsty.

I wasn't sure what that meant, but he winked at me when he said it. I think it must have been code. Grandpa was in a war where they had to use code.

Grandpa and Madge liked to hold hands, and I even saw them kiss. Lulu said that Madge had passed out and Grandpa Dub was giving her CPR. Madge passed out a lot. They got married in Las Vegas and moved to Florida to practice CPR.

After that we went through nannies faster than Belly could strip naked. I heard my uncle Max say that once. There was Jenny, Heather,

Patty, Maggie, Judy, Amy, and Sue. Sue forgot me in the grocery store once. My sisters loved almost all of our nannies, but they all seemed like Miss America contestants to me. I used to imagine them saying things like, "Hello, I'm Sue and I'm from Kansas, the Sunflower State. Although I have a very busy life riding the unicycle, picking up litter alongside the high-ways, and rescuing abandoned kittens, I still find the time to brush my teeth for two minutes every morning and every night."

I got used to playing alone while my sisters played with the "nanny of the month."

That's what Uncle Max called them. Uncle Max is my favorite uncle. He's my only uncle, but even if he weren't, he'd still be my favorite. He likes it when I walk on his back to crack it. It's my job because Lulu and India are too big and Belly is too little. Uncle Max says I'm perfect.

One rainy Monday I was coloring with Belly on the living-room floor. I was coloring a Keith Haring picture in my new pop art coloring book. Belly was actually coloring on the living-room floor. I was getting ready to tell on her when the doorbell rang, and Housman, our dog, started to bark and ran upstairs. Housman isn't like other dogs. He runs away from the door and hides in my bedroom when the doorbell rings. Mom answered the front door, and a man shook her hand. When she invited him inside, I saw that he had a bald head and wore glasses like mine, the dark-framed kind that make a person look very smart and serious. I once saw a whole article about architects and their dark-framed glasses in the *New York Times*. That's when I decided that I wanted a pair.

The visiting man was wearing a button-down blue shirt that was tucked into his jeans. He had a leather belt that matched his driving moccasins. I had seen the same brown driving moccasins in the L.L. Bean catalog last month. They looked even better in real life. The bald man wore them without socks, and his ankles were tan and had hair on them.

Lulu had run out of her room to see who was at the door. She always thinks that the telephone and doorbell are going to be for her. She recorded our answering-machine message. It says, "Hello. You've reached the Dalinger family. Lulu's not home right now. Please leave *me* a message."

Mom started to introduce the bald man to us, when he politely interrupted and said, "Oh, please call me the manny. It's what kids have always called me, and now it's become my stage name. Like Cher or Madonna or Charo. Or you can call me by my J. Lo name, T. Man. Or Puff Manny."

I wondered if Manny was short for Manuel. He didn't look Latino.

Mom continued introducing the manny to us. India curtsied when she shook his hand. India had started curtsying after she watched *Gone with the Wind* on television. She's named after one of the characters. Belly curtsied too. I just shook his hand and noticed his fancy watch with the brown leather band. After we were introduced, Mom told us that the bald man was going to spend the day with us and that if things worked out, he would be our new nanny.

A man might be our nanny. A male nanny. A manny. No wonder that's what he wanted us to call him. This was the most exciting thing that had ever happened to me. I wanted to rush to the bathroom to pee, but I didn't want to miss Lulu's reaction to the news of the man nanny.

I waited for Lulu to have a fit.

She did.

Lulu put her hands on her hips and huffed, "I bet he doesn't know how to brush hair or paint fingernails."

I whispered the word "bladder," and she ran screaming from the room. Then I danced around in circles like a circus monkey, until I realized everybody was watching me.

Mom wrote down her cell phone number for the manny and said that she'd be back early in the afternoon. I hugged her around the waist as hard as I could to show how appreciative I was. She started walking out the door while I was still clinging to her. I finally let go as she entered the garage. Actually, she had to pry me off.

The manny picked Belly up and we waved good-bye to Mom through the kitchen window. Instead of watching Mom drive away, Belly stared at the manny while she waved.

"Let's color!" the manny screamed like he was five years old. Belly jumped because it had scared her, but then she started laughing and grabbed the manny's cheeks and squeezed them until he looked like a puffer fish.

I bet the manny was an artist and he'd come to teach me abstract expressionism. I don't know what that is exactly, but Mom likes it. Or maybe he'd pretend to be my butler, and I could call him Jeeves and he could bring me milk and Oreos. Or he spoke six languages and knew lots of famous people, like Donald Trump or Weird Al Yankovic.

The manny sat down on the floor, cleaned up Belly's mess, and began coloring with me. He colored a lot of things red. He said his favorite color was red because he got a present once that was inside a red Saks Fifth Avenue box. I've never been to Saks Fifth Avenue, but I think red is my favorite color too. The manny was really good at staying in the lines. I watched his hands while he colored. He didn't have any dirt underneath his fingernails. I bet he gets manicures like the movie stars do.

The manny let Belly color the top of his head yellow. It looked like he was wearing a cheese pancake.

When I needed a different crayon, I said, "Hey, cheese head, could you please pass me the purple?"

"Crazy cheese head," said Belly, and then she laughed and rolled around on the ground like it was the funniest thing she'd ever heard.

The manny laughed so hard that he snorted.

When we were done coloring, the manny pulled mixing bowls out of the cabinet and let Belly and me make potions. Belly loves to mix different things together. Vinegar and Gummy Bears. Ranch dressing and sugar. Olive oil and flour. She calls them potions. I like making potions too, but I pretend that I'm just helping Belly.

Lulu says that I'm too old to make potions. I wish I could make a disappearing potion.

While Belly and I mixed up a maple syrup and rainbow sprinkles potion, India and the manny made us a surprise lunch. They told us not to look in the kitchen, but Belly and I peeked anyway. The manny and India were using microwave-popcorn bags on their heads like chef hats. Lulu was sitting at the kitchen table listening to her headset and scribbling something into a three-ring binder. She looked up every once in a while and rolled her eyes in disgust at India and the manny.

"You're going to get butter in your hair," Lulu grumbled.

"I don't have any hair," said the manny.

"I wasn't talking to you," Lulu snarled, and turned up the volume on her headset, so that even we could hear Celine Dion belting out the *Titanic* theme song.

When we fight in the car, Mom pretends that she's Celine Dion. She moves her head around and pounds on her chest and wails to the tune of the *Titanic* song, "Near. Far. No fighting in the car." It makes us stop fighting and start laughing, except for Lulu. She always yells, "Don't make fun of Celine." She calls her by her first name like they're friends.

The manny threw an old sheet over the kitchen table, and I ran to get a flashlight from underneath my bed. The manny served us lunch underneath the table, and we could see only by flashlight. It was like eating in a tent. Each of our plates had a peanut butter and banana sandwich cut into fourths, sliced carrots with ranch dressing, and a handful of popcorn. The manny even brought Housman's food bowl underneath there so that he could eat with us. We sat close together underneath the table so Lulu wouldn't kick any of us. Lulu ate her lunch sitting at the table and pretended to be swinging her legs to her music, but I think she was trying to hit us. She screamed and took her lunch into the other room when Belly stuck a cold carrot between her toes. We all laughed, but not out loud. We covered our mouths and shook-laughed, the same way Grandma did during Belly's nursery school fall pageant. The children sang "This Little Light of Mine," and Belly held her dress above her head every time they sang, "Hide it under a bushel? No! I'm gonna let it shine." Grandma had to leave the auditorium, but we could still hear her laughing from our seats.

We stayed underneath the table all after-noon, painting pictures with watercolors. India painted a butterfly. Belly painted shapes, but they looked more like blobs. Then she fell asleep in the manny's kindergarten-style lap. The manny and I painted portraits of each other. He was easy to paint. His head was just a circle with little ears on the sides. His portrait of me made me look really strong and muscular. He even put a superhero cape on me.

We were still underneath the table when Mom came home. She pretended she couldn't find us. We huddled close together like she was an escaped convict who had broken into our house and was looking for us. Lulu, who had spent the entire afternoon in the living room listening to her headset and writing in her binder, stomped across the kitchen floor in her bare feet and ripped the sheet off of the table to reveal the four of us huddled together. We screamed at the top of our lungs, and so did Mom. Lulu screamed too, but it wasn't out of fun. It was more like the "Aaargh!" that Charlie Brown screams every time Lucy pulls away the football in the "Peanuts" comic strip in the Sunday paper.

Lulu put her arms straight to her sides and marched toward her room. She was trying to be so dramatic that she accidentally dropped her binder, and papers flew everywhere. She scrambled for them, but I picked one up and saw that she had been making a numbered list. Number one said, "It's a health code violation to let children eat on the floor." She snatched the paper from my hands, glared at me, and huffed into her room.

India told me that when I was really little, Lulu had gotten a nanny named Amy fired by telling Mom and Dad that she didn't think I liked her because I cried every time Amy came over and Mom and Dad left. India said the truth was that Amy wouldn't let Lulu watch *Jeopardy* until all of her homework was done. It made Lulu mad.

"Did I cry when she came over and Mom and Dad left?" I asked India.

"Of course you did, you were two years old. You cried when anyone left. You even cried when Housman went outside to pee."

"I did not," I argued.

"You did too," said India. "It's documented in one of our family photo albums." She ran over to the bookshelves, pulled down a burgundy photo album, and began flipping through it. She stopped and pulled out a picture of me when I was two years old, standing and crying by the back door. On the other side of the glass was Housman, peeing in the yard. India's story was true. I hoped her story about Lulu's getting a nanny fired wasn't true.

At five o'clock, after we'd made s'mores in the fireplace, it was time for the manny to leave. Mom asked us to go play in our rooms so that she could talk to him privately. Ms. Grant has spoken to me privately at school. It means you're in trouble. India took Belly into the bathroom to wash the paint off her face. I pretended to leave but hid behind the couch to see if Mom was going to make the manny write sentences: *I will not let Belly color my head yellow.* One time when Ms. Grant spoke to me privately, she made me write "I will not comb my hair during class" on a piece of paper twenty-five times. I thought it was fun. I didn't tell Ms. Grant, but I like to practice my handwriting.

Instead of making him write sentences, Mom told the manny that she would like to hire him as our nanny. I let out a "whoopee" and then remembered that I was hiding. I growled a little and barked so that they would think that it was Housman. Mom and the manny kept talking. The manny told Mom that he never really stayed in one place for very long because he loved adventures. I bet he's been bungee jumping and skinny-dipping. Those are two things that I'm not adventurous enough to do. I guess Lulu won't have to work too hard to get him to leave. She hates adventure. She won't even let Dad push her on the swings. The manny also told Mom that he understood if she found a nanny who could commit for a longer time.

Mom said, "I'll keep an eye out, but for now I think that it would be great to have you working with the children." Then he and Mom began to talk about pay and schedules.

Now the manny comes to our house every day of the week, except for Saturdays and Sundays. He said that Saturdays and Sundays are the days that he works as a fashion runway model in Paris. Lulu said that he was kidding and that he probably just does his laundry and dishes on the weekend like everybody else.

Lulu tries her hardest not to smile or laugh when the manny is around. She usually just sits and writes in her three-ring binder. She told India that she is keeping a log of all of the things the manny does that she thinks are going to scar us for life. She said that either she'll use it now to reason with Mom and Dad, or she'll use it later in therapy.

She calls it "The Manny Files." I saw the title page, and the words were written really big like in one of Dad's important documents.

Yesterday Lulu devoted a whole page in "The Manny Files" to inappropriate things that the manny thought were funny, like when he jumped on the trampoline with us. He laughed when I spun so fast that drool came out of my mouth. Drool always comes out of my mouth when we jump on the trampoline. Usually everyone squeals "Gross" and won't come near me. They never laugh. The manny even cleaned up my slobber with the bottom of his sock.

Lulu just said, "That's disgusting," and scribbled some notes.

The manny can do flips. He said that when he was little, his dad used to take him to the doughnut shop and make him do back hand-springs for all of his friends. They always got free doughnuts.

I want to go to a doughnut shop with him.

He taught Lulu how to do a back handspring. She wrote down "Back handspring" in her "Things I Can Do" book, right underneath "Deliver puppies" and "Play the piano." She told me that the manny really didn't help her very much, but I could tell that he had by the way he grunted when he spotted her.

3 I See London, I See France

Lulu has been taking piano lessons for two years. I've never done anything for two years, unless you count wetting the bed. I did that when I was three and four. When I stopped wetting the bed, Dad bought me Egyptian cotton sheets. They were just like the ones at the St. Regis Hotel. I've never been to the St. Regis Hotel, but Grandma told me that they serve excellent room-service omelets, and that it's near Saks Fifth Avenue. The carpets are red.

Lulu has her spring piano recital on Friday. She has been practicing two songs that she has to play solo. At school *solo* means "all by yourself, without the help of your neighbor." I learned that when I asked my friend Sarah how to spell the word *committee* during a spelling test.

"Ahem." Ms. Grant cleared her throat and stared at me from her desk. She asked, "Keats, is there a problem I can help you with?"

I said, "No. I was telling Sarah that I thought

the bun in your hair made you look pretty."

Ms. Grant spoke to me privately after school. She said she was "fixin'" to call my mother and father, but instead she made me write "I will work solo on tests" on a sheet of paper twenty-five times.

One night at dinner Lulu announced that she would have top billing in the program at the piano concert. She said that she wasn't nervous about being on stage all by herself, but I could tell that she was. When India said, "All by yourself? Nobody else? All eyes on you?" Lulu turned white.

The manny told Lulu to wear lots of feathers and sequins like Liberace. India told me that Liberace is a fancy French cheese that is served with red wine. I guess you wear feathers and sequins when you eat it.

I'm going to order it the next time I'm at a fancy restaurant.

Lulu told the manny to mind his own business. Mom didn't hear it. If she had, Lulu would have been grounded. We're not allowed to speak to people (especially adults) the way Lulu spoke to the manny. I wanted to tell on her, but I stopped being a tattletale last year after I told Mom that Dad drank straight out of the milk carton. Dad called me a tattletale for a week.

Instead Mom asked the manny if he wanted to come to the piano recital with the rest of my family. He said that he couldn't wait to start a standing ovation. Lulu got mad and promised that she would move to Kentucky and change her name to Spatula if the manny embarrassed her.

I hope he does.

The next day I went with the manny to pick up Lulu from her piano lesson. I usually stay in the car when we pick Lulu up from her piano lessons, because the piano teacher's house smells like cats. She has eight scraggly-looking cats. Some of them are missing clumps of hair. One black-and-white fluffy one raised the hair on its back and hissed at me one time, and Mom had to pick me up to keep me safe.

I didn't want to miss anything the manny did, so I went in the house this time. I stood right in the doorway and behind the manny. A cinnamon-colored cat rubbed up against my legs, while the black-and-white fluffy one stared at me from the top of the bookshelves. I kept an eye on him because he looked like he might pounce at any moment. The manny asked Lulu's piano teacher if he could set up a booth after the recital and charge money for Lulu's autographed sheet music. Lulu rolled her eyes and walked to the car like she was in a huff, but I could see by the way her hair jiggled that she was pleased with herself. Mom says Lulu's pleased with herself a lot. The piano teacher giggled and batted her eyelashes at the manny. We left the house just as a catfight was starting in the living room underneath the piano. We could hear the piano teacher trying to break up the fight until we were inside the Eurovan.

On the car ride home Lulu told the manny that she would prefer it if he didn't get out of the car when he dropped her off or picked her up from activities like piano lessons or origami. (She once made a life-size horse out of folded paper.) The manny turned to Lulu and hissed like a cat. Lulu pretended not to hear him. She was writing in "The Manny Files."

Lulu looked up from "The Manny Files" and caught me watching her writing in it. Without saying a word, she pointed up at the manny and then took her hand and made a throat-slicing sign, like she wanted to cut off his head. The manny didn't see her. He was watching the road and waving to pedestrians he didn't know to see who would wave back. I stuck my tongue out at Lulu, but I think she could still tell that I was worried.

At dinner that night Lulu told Mom and Dad that a boy from her class named Theodosius used to play the trumpet in the school band with a boy the manny knew. Theodosius said that the manny went to see the boy's band concert last year and showed up with a conductor's wand that he pretended to lead the band with. During the "Go, fight, win!" finale, whenever the band would pause, the manny would jump up and yell, "Go, Fight, Win!" Theodosius told Lulu that the boy now lives in Mexico, is called Mario, and plays the clarinet.

I wish my name were Theodosius.

Today was recital day. Mom curled Lulu's hair, while India tried to put together an ensemble of clothes for Lulu to wear to her debut. India likes to say that she wears ensembles, not outfits. She says that ensembles are more sophisticated. I think that means R-rated. India chose a purple knee-length dress. The manny said that purple was a good choice because you wouldn't be able to see sweat marks in the armpits. Lulu screamed. She hates the word *armpit*. She really didn't think it was funny when the manny showed up in a shirt that was the same shade of purple as her dress. He said that he wanted his outfit to match hers so that everyone would know whom he was there to watch.

"It's called an ensemble," said India.

The manny said that if their "ensembles" matched, it would be more convenient if Lulu decided to pull him onstage for a tap-dancing, piano-playing encore. Dad said that the manny had a brilliant sense of humor. Lulu said he was "de-minted," but I thought his breath smelled fine.

At the recital I sat next to the manny. I wore khaki pants and my blue sweater vest with a white collared shirt underneath it. The manny wore the same color of khaki pants as mine. I pointed this out to him and he smiled. He pointed out Lulu's name in the program before he shoved it into his jacket pocket. He said he was keeping it for his scrapbook. I shoved my program in my pants pocket for my scrapbook.

During the performance Lulu went to the bathroom six times while the other kids were playing their songs. Whenever she left the auditorium, she had to walk past the manny. He gave her the thumbs-up sign every time. They called Lulu's name to perform, but she was in the bathroom. They called her name two more times, but she didn't come onstage. She finally ran quickly from the side of the stage to the piano. I thought she looked beautiful under the stage lights, like a picture from Mom's *Vogue* magazines. The audience clapped politely, and she looked around the room and found us. The manny gave her the thumbs-up sign.

She pulled out the piano bench, which made a screeching noise across the floor. Some people in the audience flinched and covered their ears. She nodded to the crowd, sat down on the bench, and began to play her first song, "Mr. Bojangles." She had to start over three times. The manny turned and whispered in my ear, "She's repeating for effect, just like the Rolling Stones."

The manny always sings the Rolling Stones song "You Can't Always Get What You Want" whenever Lulu wants something that she can't have. She hates it when he sings to her. She gets red and looks like there's a scream in her that can't find its way out of her mouth.

Lulu's second song was "Imagine," by John Lennon. Dad explained the song to me. He said that it's about dreaming for a world of peace where people's differences are celebrated. At our school's last Christmas pageant my class dressed up in costumes and sang "It's a Small World After All." My best friend, Sarah, wore a Japanese kimono. I dressed up like an Eskimo, but nobody could see me. The poofy-red-haired girl dressed up like a Native American and stood in front of me. She wore a tall, feathered headdress. I picked a red feather out of the back of it and put it in my pocket. She never even knew.

Lulu played "Imagine" perfectly, with not one mistake. I saw the lady in front of me wipe a tear off her cheek. When Lulu finished, she leaped to her feet to take a dramatic bow, just like she had practiced in front of her bedroom mirror. The audience roared with applause. Then she turned sideways to bow to her teacher.

And that's when we all saw it.

The audience clapped louder and laughed a little.

Mom blushed.

Dad gasped.

India giggled.

Belly was looking for her shirt under the seats.

Lulu's dress was tucked into the back of her underwear, the ones that said TUESDAY across the tush.

India said really loudly, "Isn't this Friday?"

The manny leaned over to me and whispered, "I see London, I see France."

Then he jumped up and cheered, and so did the person next to him, and then the next, until the whole crowd was on its feet clapping wildly.

It was a standing ovation, just like the manny had promised. I thought about what color I would paint Lulu's room if I got to have it after she moved to Kentucky and changed her name to Spatula. The clapping lasted for two whole minutes, which was how long it took Lulu to figure out that her panties were showing. She quickly untucked her dress and continued to bow.

Later the piano teacher told the manny that she had never seen an ovation like it and gave him a kiss on the cheek. He turned his favorite color. Red.

We went out for ice cream after the recital. Lulu got a chocolate malt. India got a huge banana split with strawberry, chocolate, and caramel sauces. Belly got a red grape slush. Mom and Dad split a chocolate soda. The manny got chocolate chip cookie dough ice cream. I got a plain vanilla cone.

Mom and Dad were very proud and kept shaking hands with other parents who were saying nice things about Lulu's piano skills. The manny told Lulu that she was a genius to make herself so memorable to the audience like that. He said that she was just like Madonna.

The manny turned to India and said, "I can't wait until your gymnastics meet next week. Can I borrow a leotard?"

Be Interesting 4

Every year in April, Mom and Dad go on a vacation alone together to celebrate their wedding anniversary. Kids aren't allowed. Dad says that the first time he kissed Mom, he saw fireworks. Mom says that she had a spiky, colorful hairdo when she met Dad and that he was actually looking at her bangs and not fireworks. Dad had a mohawk and a leather jacket with safety pins all over it when he met Mom. That sounds dangerous.

India says that the eighties were a fashion tragedy.

This year Mom and Dad are going away to Mexico for a whole week. Lulu wants to go because she says she needs to "feed her soul," but Dad says that this trip is for romance. Lulu hates the word *romance*. Once, in a fancy restaurant, she insisted on sitting at her own table because Mom and Dad were cuddling in the booth. They had been fighting about finances the night before. Finances are the plastic cards that Mom uses to pay for groceries and clothes. I could hear them arguing through my bedroom wall. I hated it, but they made up before they went to bed. The next morning they were in their terry-cloth robes hugging each other while they waited for their coffee to brew.

Our waiter at the fancy restaurant wore a black bow tie and a white short apron around his waist. He showed me how to use the decrumber to clean off the tablecloth. I accidentally put it in my pocket and took it home. Every night after dinner I decrumb the table before Mom serves us our dessert. We don't get many crumbs because Mom only makes spaghetti. She's really good at it, but I'm not sure if she knows how to make anything else.

This morning Mom kissed us good-bye, and Dad gave each of us airplane rides on his feet before they walked us to meet the school bus. Lulu said that she wanted twenty dollars in cash instead of an airplane ride. Mom told us that when we returned from school, the manny would be here to meet us. She had made India and Lulu change the sheets in the guest room. Lulu had wanted to short-sheet the bed, but India wouldn't let her.

Mom left important telephone numbers by the telephone.

Dr. Little at the Tiny Tyke Health Office. Grandma. Pizza delivery.

The manny was going to stay with us! I had been dancing around the house since I found out, jumping off the couch and squawking like a chicken. Dad said that I was acting the same way that Belly does after she eats chocolate cake. He calls it OC. It stands for "out of control."

We waved good-bye to Mom and Dad from the bus window. Our bus driver wears a pink scarf around her neck and has curly red hair. She reminds me of the waitress at the diner that Grandma and the canasta ladies took me to once for breakfast. She talks like her too. She calls me "darlin'."

I put down the bus window and yelled, "Bring me a surprise!"

India blew kisses.

Lulu screeched, "No hugging or kissing in public."

Just then Mom and Dad kissed.

All the kids on the bus went, "Ewwwww!"

Lulu sank low into her seat as the bus drove away.

Mom and Dad were still kissing on the sidewalk.

I couldn't concentrate on anything at school that day. During choir I fell off the back of the risers while we were singing "Bye, Bye Blackbird." Mr. Strickland, our music teacher, made me sit aside and draw one hundred treble clefs on a piece of paper. He thought this was punishment, but I like drawing treble clefs. I think they're fancy.

During recess, while the other boys played kickball, I sat on top of the monkey bars with my friend Sarah. I used to play kickball, but I fell once and tore a hole in the elbow of the sweater that Grandma had knit for me from the pattern I had picked out. Now I play kickball only when I'm wearing India's hand-me-downs.

Sarah and I like to sit on top of the monkey bars and talk. Sarah says that our conversations reach a higher level up there. She also thinks that there are things more important than kickball. Like Hello Kitty and books. Sarah's room is full of books. She's the one who told me that I was named after a tragic poet who died from tuberculosis when he was twenty-five. I thought that was an awful story, but Sarah said that it was "fantastical." Sarah uses the word *fantastical* a lot. When she says it, she always lifts her hands and head with a quick snap like she just dismounted from a trapeze. I told her that the manny was going to spend the next few nights with us.

Sarah said, "I bet he lets you have cake for breakfast."

"I bet he sleeps in cashmere," I said. I had heard on National Public Radio that they fight over cashmere in Pakistan. I thought to myself that this might be the week that actually pushed Lulu over the edge and into a nervous breakdown.

Fantastical.

On the bus ride home India sat next to me. Lulu sat in front of us and let India put braids in her hair. Lulu thinks braids make her look artsy. I think they make her look like Pippi Longstocking without the fun socks.

When we pulled up to our stop, I heard Lulu whimper. I scrambled over her and peered out the window to see the manny standing at the curb wearing a big sombrero on his head and carrying a portable stereo that was playing "Mexican Hat Dance." Belly was standing next to him in a little Chihuahua costume. India and I jumped off of the bus and started dancing around the manny. Lulu sat on the bus and pretended that it wasn't her stop.

The manny yelled into the bus, "*Hola*, Lulu! *Qué pasa?*"

She glared at him but grabbed her backpack and trudged off the bus, blowing air kisses to friends and holding her hand up to her ear like a telephone.

"Call me," she mouthed without a sound to her best friend, Margo.

"Bye, darlin'," said the bus driver. I couldn't tell if she was talking to Lulu or to the manny.

The bus drove away with all of our classmates' hands and faces pressed against the windows, staring at us. Lulu walked ten feet in front of the rest of us all the way home.

The manny sang, "'There she was just a-walkin' down the street, singin' "Do wah diddy diddy dum diddy do."'" She turned around and looked like she was going to scream, but instead she ran the rest of the way home. India and I laughed and made the manny teach us the whole song.

When we got home, Lulu was already scribbling in "The Manny Files." The manny made us a snack. Homemade tortilla chips and fresh guacamole. It was really good. He told me that he'd give me free meals next year when he was a chef in New York City at a restaurant called Lay Burning Down. India told me later that it was called Le Bernardin.

Lulu closed her notebook and helped me with my cursive letters, while the manny and India had a multiplying contest. India won, but

I think the manny let her win on purpose.

We had tacos for dinner that night. The manny said that if we couldn't go to Mexico, Mexico would have to come to us. After dinner we all brushed our teeth. I have an electric toothbrush that sends ultrasounds into your teeth and fights decay. I circled it in a catalog and Grandma got it for me for my birthday.

When I unwrapped it, Grandma said, "Keats, I'm glad that you take pride in your smile. You know that beauty is only skin deep, but ugly is all the way through," and then she laughed like a witch.

Mom grumbled.

When the flossing and brushing were complete, we went into our bedrooms and then ran right back out into the hall screaming with joy.

"There's a piñata hanging from my ceiling," I shouted.

"Mine too!" squealed India as she hugged herself and spun around in a circle.

Belly just jumped up and down in her fake silk PRINCESSES OF DISNEYLAND nightgown.

Lulu jumped up and down too but stopped when she saw that we had noticed.

We all ran into one another's rooms to see what was hanging from the ceiling. Lulu had a horse dangling from her ceiling. India had a butterfly.

Belly had a pig. I had a big red-and-gold king's crown. The girls picked up their old twirling batons and immediately began smashing their piñatas open. The manny held Belly up so she could reach. Tootsie Rolls, SweeTarts, and plastic gold coins came crashing down on them like confetti during the New Year's celebration on television. The girls stashed the candy in their top drawers, underneath their underwear. Mine was too beautiful to hit. I climbed into bed and watched the light dance on the gold paper hanging from the crown. The manny stood outside our bedroom windows and serenaded us with "La Cucaracha" in a Spanish accent.

Lulu yelled out the window that she was going to call the police.

This worried me, so I ran to India's room to ask her if the manny was doing something illegal. She told me that Lulu was only kidding and that the police couldn't arrest the manny for singing in our yard unless he was drunk. I don't think he was drunk. The margaritas that he made us were alcohol-free.

On the way back to my room I decided that if Lulu drove the manny away, I would kidnap her favorite stuffed bunny and mail it back to her one piece at a time. An ear. A nose. A cotton tail.

The next morning I woke up to the manny

singing, "'Schoolboy. Time to wake up and go to school so you can learn something so you can grow up and be somebody.'" He sounded like Frank Sinatra live at the Sahara. Uncle Max listens to Frank Sinatra in his Honda Accord. I sprang out of bed, got dressed, and ran to the kitchen. The manny was standing there in gray flannel pajamas and *cashmere* socks, flipping pancakes high into the air. Belly was next to him, in her pink tutu and no top, flipping American cheese slices in a Tupperware bowl.

The manny had set the table, complete with a centerpiece of rulers and number two pencils sticking out of a silver mint julep cup. I poured milk into all of the glasses except for Belly's. Belly is lactose intolerant. I think she's just intolerable. That's the word Ms. Grant uses when I ask to go to the bathroom too many times in one day.

After I poured apple juice into Belly's glass, the manny began serving our pancakes. Instead of bringing us perfectly round pancakes like Dad does, the manny served pancakes that were shaped like letters and animals. He used Dad's coffee cream pitcher to pour the shapes. He kept closing one eye and holding up his thumb in front of his face like an artist. India called him Pablo Pancake-asso.

Belly's pancakes were shaped like rabbits and ducks. She quickly bit the heads off and laughed. Syrup dripped from the corners of her mouth like blood.

India's pancakes spelled her name.

Mine were shaped in the life cycle of the frog, from tadpole to full-grown frog.

Lulu screamed when she saw her pancakes. They spelled the word *belch*. She refused to eat them and demanded that the manny trade his pancakes with hers. His spelled the word *hunk*.

I told the manny that the pancakes were incredible. *Incredible* is another one of Sarah's words that she uses to describe things like movies, books, and ice cream flavors. The manny told me that when his cookbook comes out next year, the pancake recipe will be in it. The manny has a lot going on "next year."

We ate our pancakes and ran as fast as we could to the bus stop. India couldn't wait to tell her friends about the piñatas. Lulu said she was running to get away from the manny.

As the bus pulled to the curb to pick us up, we heard the manny's voice yelling, "Wait, you forgot your lunches!" We looked back to see him barreling toward the bus on my bike, which was much too small for him. He wobbled a little bit, and the lunch bags looked heavy hanging on the handlebars. Belly was right beside him on her Hot Wheels, wearing her ladybug helmet. The manny was still wearing his flannel pajamas and cashmere socks. He wasn't wearing any shoes. He handed us the lunches he had packed in old shopping bags.

Tiffany and Company. Barneys. Bergdorf Goodman.

India said, "These seem really heavy. What's in them?"

The manny said, "You'll have to wait until lunch to find out."

"See you after school, fool." I smiled at the manny.

"See ya round town, clown," he said back to me.

"Catch you on the down low," said India.

"See ya. Wouldn't wanna be ya. If you were in the zoo, I wouldn't free ya," said Lulu without a smile. We got on the bus, and I walked too close to the back of Lulu. She hates it when people step on her heels.

The bus doors closed behind us, and we scanned the aisles for some seats. The whole bus looked at us like we were a group of circus clowns at an orphanage. Everybody wanted me to sit with them. When the bus started to move, I glanced out the window. The manny was alongside the bus on my bike, leaning forward and gnashing his teeth, pretending to be racing with us. Lulu pulled out her three-ring binder and wrote it all down. I tried to peek over her shoulder to see what she was writing, but she covered it with her hand and said, "He'll be gone by summer."

I looked at India, who scrunched up her face and shook her head no. She said, "Mom and Dad like him. Don't worry about it."

But I can't help it. I worry about everything. Asteroids hitting the earth. The deterioration of the ozone layer. Head lice.

At lunchtime I walked into the cafeteria and searched the room for an empty seat. I walked by a boy named Craig. He put his hand down on the seat next to him and said that I couldn't sit there. I didn't want to sit there anyway. Craig is in my class and doesn't like me. At the beginning of the school year he told me that my shoes were too clean. I told him that his shoes were too little. I thought it was a good comeback at the time, but he just laughed and kicked dirt on my shoes. Sarah helped me clean them off. She said he was a Neanderthal. India told me that a Neanderthal is a person with one big eyebrow instead of two and a hairy back. Dad's a Neanderthal.

When it's my turn to kick in kickball, Craig always says, "He can't kick. Everybody move closer." The whole kickball game moves in closer. They move back out when it's Sarah's turn to kick.

She can kick it over their heads.

I spotted Sarah standing up and shaking her hands in the air like she was waving in an airplane. I went in for a landing on the orange stool next to hers. Sarah asked if I wanted a biscuit. It was really a cookie, but Sarah's mom is from England, where they call cookies "biscuits," moms "mums," and toilets "loos." I like going over to Sarah's house because her mom always asks if I'd like a "spot of milk." One time I drank way more than a spot and had to race to the loo. Sarah's mom had hundreds of little perfume bottles on silver trays all over the bathroom counter. They looked like they had fallen out of a treasure chest. Blue, yellow, and orange liquids in the fanciest crystal bottles that I had ever seen. I picked up a little bottle that said TABU and misted my face with it. It stung my eyes and tasted like shampoo, but I didn't care.

When I walked back out into the kitchen, Sarah's mom said, "Oh, my word. Somebody smells gorgeous."

I tried not to blush.

I gladly took a biscuit from Sarah and reached into my Barneys lunch bag for something to trade with her. I pulled out a cheese and bacon sandwich (my favorite), a split-open pomegranate, a small bag of Gummy Bears, carrots, and a whole coconut, still in its shell. The coconut had a note written on it with black Sharpie. It said, BE INTERESTING. I think the manny put the coconut in my lunch to be funny. I looked across the cafeteria and spotted India. I held up the coconut and smiled. She held up a whole pineapple. Sarah wanted to trade for the coconut, even though she couldn't eat it. She settled for the Gummy Bears.

On the bus ride home Lulu documented more "misdeeds" into "The Manny Files." He had sent a bottle of fish food in her lunch bag with a note that said, "Have fun in your *school*." She turned to me and said, "I know you like him, but don't you think that he might be a little mentally unbalanced?"

"I think he's interesting," I said, holding the coconut in my lap.

Just as I uttered those words, I glanced out the bus window and saw the manny and Belly wearing chauffeur hats and holding three poster board signs. Across each sign in big black capital letters were our names: LULU DALINGER. INDIA

DALINGER. KEATS DALINGER. He was like a limousine driver picking up businessmen that he didn't know from the airport. Lulu started a new page in "The Manny Files."

I Scotch-taped the sign with my name on it to my bedroom door.

I put the coconut on my dresser.

5 All We Are Saying . . . Is Give Peas a Chance

On one of the nights that the manny was staying with us, we had to take Belly to the emergency room. We have taken Belly to the emergency room once before, when she was a year and a half old, or eighteen months in baby age. It was before she could talk, or at least before we could understand her, and she wouldn't stop crying. Mom tried rocking her, singing to her, giving her warm milk, and even putting her on top of the dryer. She said that Belly liked the noise and gentle shaking. I thought about suggesting inside the dryer but knew that it would be inappropriate with Mom so upset. I learned the word *inappropriate* when I stood up at school and told a knock-knock joke that I heard my uncle Max tell my dad. I didn't understand the joke, but it had the word *brassiere* in it. I guess that my teacher understood it.

When the dryer trick didn't work, my dad called the hospital. We rushed Belly to the emergency room. Lulu and India were sobbing but stopped when they saw that the waiting room had old *Highlights* magazines. I had always dreamed of returning Belly to the hospital, but now that we were actually doing it, I was a little scared.

I held her hand.

The emergency-room doctor came into the room and said, "First let's strip her down to her diaper." He untied one shoe and then the other and took them off of her fat raisin feet. She immediately stopped crying.

My mom and dad both looked at each other.

"She stopped," Mom said, relieved.

"Why did she stop?" Dad asked the doctor.

The doctor gave Mom and Dad an annoyed look and said, "I think her shoes were tied too tightly and were hurting her. Now, if you'll excuse me, I have lives to save."

I don't remember if the doctor really said the last part, but that's the way Lulu tells the story.

That was the night we took Belly to the hospital for emergency shoe removal.

This time was different. We had all finished our homework and were having dinner. The manny made India's favorite: macaroni and cheese (spaghetti noodles for Belly), biscuits with honey, and peas. I was just finishing my macaroni and cheese. I eat the food I like worst first and the food I like best last. This way the last taste you have in your mouth is the best. Who wants to taste peas all night long? Tonight I started with peas, then biscuits, and finally macaroni and cheese. I was just about to get the decrumber so that I could clean the table for dessert, when the manny said, "Do you hear that whistling?"

We all stopped talking. At first we could hear only Housman's dog snores underneath the table. Then we heard a quiet whistle. We looked around and all at once figured out that the whistling was coming from Belly's nose. She had shoved a pea up it and now it was stuck. We weren't surprised that it took us so long to notice. Belly always has something green hanging out of her nose.

Belly wasn't upset at all. She didn't even cry. Instead she said to the manny, "Are you mad at me?"

The manny said, "No. Of course not, but why would you shove anything up your nose?"

I started to say, "Lulu shoves her finger up hers," but I didn't.

"Because I'm crazy," said Belly. "Aren't I crazy?"

Belly gets away with everything just because she's the youngest. When she painted the tail of our neighbor's cat green, Mom just shook her head and said, "You're so crazy." When Belly put on Mom's lipstick and practiced kissing the bathroom mirror, Dad just laughed and said, "You are one crazy baby." *Crazy* is Belly's favorite word. Now Belly always says this when she's done something wrong and she doesn't want to get into trouble. She is the youngest criminal ever to plead insane.

The manny said that next year he was going to go to school to be a nurse, and he grabbed a toothpick and tried to get the pea out. Belly wouldn't stop wiggling, so the manny said we'd have to go to the hospital. We left our uneaten portions of dinner on the table and loaded into the Volkswagen Eurovan to go to the emergency room. The manny asked Lulu and India to roll down their windows, stick out their heads, and make "woo-ooo" siren sounds. They did. I held my arms out of the sunroof and turned a flashlight on and off. The manny pretended to be talking on a CB radio. "We're headed in with a pea that's been attacked by a nostril. I've seen this before, but never quite this bad. It looks like the pea might need surgery, if it can be saved at all. It looks pretty smashed. The tragic part is that the rest of this poor pea's family died earlier tonight." Belly laughed, even though she probably didn't understand it.

When we arrived at the hospital, Lulu and India raced into the lobby and began flipping through *Highlights* magazines. They said things like, "Oh, I love this one," and, "I hope we get to stay longer than we did last time." It was like a homecoming. Lulu got bored with trying to find the hidden pictures and began writing in "The Manny Files."

I went into the examining room with the manny and Belly. The doctor came in and removed the pea from Belly's nose with long metal tweezers. When he pulled it out and held it on the end of his finger to show Belly, she grabbed it and stuffed it into her mouth. The manny said she was sweet to put it out of its misery like that.

On the car ride home Lulu scolded, "I can't believe you let her eat that pea. Why did you do that, Mirabelle?" She calls her Mirabelle when she pretends to be Mom.

"Because I'm crazy."

The manny started singing, "All we are saying . . . is give peas a chance."

After several days of finding unusual useless objects in our lunches and returning from school to find a spectacle awaiting us at the curb, Mom and Dad came back from Mexico. Lulu's "The Manny Files" was nearly ready for a second notebook. I caught her smiling once while she was writing in it. I told her that I could tell by her smile that she liked the nutty things the manny did. She said that she was smiling because she was fantasizing about Mom and Dad's horrified faces when they learned that the manny had worn a tutu over his jeans one day when he met the bus. Or that he'd juggled eggs in the kitchen and dropped one on the floor. Or that he called our bus driver "sweet potato" to her face. I grabbed the notebook and tried to take it from her, but she pulled it back out of my hands. It left a paper cut on my thumb. She ran to her room and hid "The Manny Files."

We spent the entire Saturday morning

preparing for Mom and Dad's evening arrival at the airport. The manny woke us up early, except for Belly. He said that we could watch an hour of cartoons, but then we would have to start our chores. We were going to make the house spotless before Mom and Dad got home. That's why we let Belly sleep. The last time she tried to help us clean the house, we had to spend an hour trying to free Housman's tail from the vacuum cleaner.

Lulu, India, the manny, and I sat and watched cartoons while we ate bowl after crunchy bowl of Frosted Flakes.

"*They're grrrrreat,*" said the manny with milk dripping from his lower lip.

"*You're disssgusting!*" mimicked Lulu.

The manny likes cartoons. I think his favorite is Tweety Bird. He laughs so hard that he snorts whenever Tweety says, "I did! I did! I did taw a puddy tat." The manny's head is sort of shaped like Tweety Bird's. He said, "Thufferin' thuckatash," when I pointed it out to him.

Lulu was in charge of bathrooms and floors.

India was in charge of dusting and dishes.

I was in charge of aesthetics, which meant that I had to make the rooms beautiful. I would have to choose the most perfect flower arrangement for the dining-room table and the most interesting art books for the coffee table. The manny told me that aesthetics were very important because they could make our living room—which was usually filled with stuffed animals, plastic groceries from Belly's toy shopping cart, and scattered puzzle pieces—seem a little more elegant.

He said, "The person who is in charge of aesthetics needs to be sensitive to both art and beauty."

I was born for this role.

I ran to my room and changed into my T-shirt from the Museum of Modern Art for inspiration, the one that Uncle Max had given me. He calls the Museum of Modern Art "MoMA." Uncle Max is an oil painter and dreams of having his work hang in MoMA. Right now he hangs his paintings in his basement. They are mostly of naked people reading books. Lulu thinks that he should paint more puppies and horses and things that match people's couches. She hates naked people.

India told me that Lulu probably wears her swimsuit in the shower.

While we each began our assigned jobs, the manny began putting away all the toys that didn't find their way back into the toy closet while Mom was away. Mom makes us pick up our own toys. We hardly ever get the fun jobs like bathrooms and dishes.

Belly woke up and walked into the living room wearing nothing but a diaper and carrying her dolly, Tina, which had no head. A few months earlier Belly and Tina were riding in the back of Mom's Volvo. Belly likes to play with the automatic windows.

Up. Down. Up. Down. Up. Down.

She lifted Tina's head up to the window so that Tina could see an airplane that was flying overhead. She decided to let Tina hang in the window for a little bit. She rolled the window up almost all the way, so that Tina hung there with her head on the outside of the car and her body on the inside. Then Belly laughed and pressed the window button up until the window was completely closed and Tina's head popped off. Mom didn't even notice until she looked in her rearview mirror and saw Tina's head bouncing down the road behind the car. Mom spun around and looked into the backseat.

Belly said, "I'm crazy," and shrugged her shoulders as if to say, *I can't help it.*

I think it's creepy that Belly still carries Tina's headless body around.

The manny calls the doll DecapiTina.

Belly and DecapiTina planted themselves on the couch, snuggled under a blanket, and watched cartoons.

Whenever we would finish a job, the manny would inspect. He'd cross his arms and say, "Hmmm," running his finger along surfaces to see if they had been cleaned properly. He thought Lulu did a beautiful job on the bathroom. Everything gleamed like capped teeth. Shiny faucets. Shiny toilet. Shiny floor.

The manny said, "This bathroom is so clean we could eat right on the floor."

We did.

We had a picnic lunch, complete with fried chicken and lemonade, right on the bathroom floor. Normally Lulu would never eat in the bathroom, but she did because she was pleased with herself. She grinned the same way that she had when she was named Typist of the Year at last year's awards assembly at school. Fifty-seven words per minute.

India also got rave reviews for her spotless dishes and thorough dusting. In Dad's office she dusted each of the little knickknacks that he'd collected from around the world: Buddha, Venetian blown glass, Mardi Gras beads.

When it was time for my evaluation, I requested that everyone sit on the couch with the coffee table in front of it. They had already seen the arrangement that I made for the dining-room table—willow sticks and lavender lilacs from the backyard. India had hovered over it like a butterfly, smelling the lilacs.

Now it was time to show them my masterpiece. I had spent half an hour looking through our library and choosing which books to place stacked on the coffee table. I had chosen seven books.

I began to explain.

"The books on a family's coffee table say a lot about who they are and what they think. This was a very stressful job for me because I needed to represent every member of the family and not just myself."

Lulu rolled her eyes and breathed too loudly, like a scuba diver on the Discovery Channel.

I picked up the first book.

I went on, "The book that represents me is *A Feng Shui Life.*"

Mom had taken a feng shui class last summer at the community art center. Her teacher wore too many necklaces and smelled like an Indian restaurant. Mom explained to me that the way a room is arranged and decorated affects the energy fields of the people who live in the room. Every night when she returned from class, she would move our furniture around.

Our beds away from windows. Candles in every room. Mirrors everywhere.

Lulu loved the mirrors.

I told Mom that I could feel the energy opening up in the room, but I'm not sure if that's what I really felt. Earlier that morning I had used Q-tips to clean my ears and pulled out the biggest piece of wax I'd ever seen. I think that I could just hear better.

I kept the earwax in a jar under my bed for two days. I had trouble sleeping when it was under my bed. I think it closed my feng shui energy fields. I ended up throwing it out.

"I chose this coffee table book about Oscar de la Renta to represent India. He has great style and taste and knows how to dress women."

I had read that quote from a lady named Diana Vreeland on page 43 of the book. I don't know who Diana Vreeland is, but in her picture she is sitting in a room where everything is "the perfect red." India smiled and adjusted her blue-and-yellow sarong that she was wearing. Mom and Dad had brought it to her from Bali.

Lulu leaned forward and said, "Which book represents me?"

I picked up a book called *Your Moody Preteen* and began to smile when I saw the horrified look on Lulu's face.

"I'm just kidding," I said.

Everyone, except for Lulu, began to laugh.

"The real book that I chose for you is this one. It's called *Great Pianists of Our Time.*"

"Am I in it?" asked Lulu.

I showed them all of the books that I had carefully chosen. *The New Yorker Book of Dog Cartoons* for Dad. *Moroccan Gardens* for Mom. *The Very Hungry Caterpillar* for Belly. I couldn't find a book about headless dolls.

"Who is the last book for?" asked India, pointing to a tattered old children's book that was lying next to the six glossy tabletop books that I had just presented.

I reached for the last book on the table and said, "This book represents the manny."

I held it up.

Mary Poppins.

Please Don't Have 7 Any More Children! J/K

We spent the rest of the afternoon making welcome-home signs for Mom and Dad. Lulu made a banner that was twelve feet long to hang in the front hallway so that it would be the first thing they saw when they walked into the house. She used a paintbrush to paint the words THANK GOODNESS YOU'RE HOME across the long white butcher paper. She isn't very subtle. I learned the word *subtle* from Ms. Grant. She told me to be more subtle at the beginning of the school year when I grabbed the front of my jeans and started jumping up and down and said, "I have to pee like a racehorse." I had heard Uncle Max say this at the movies once when he'd finished his extra-jumbo soda. Now I just raise my hand and Ms. Grant knows that I have to pee like a racehorse without my having to tell her.

While the manny added carrots to the stew that was brewing on the stove, India, Belly, and I made signs to hold up at the airport. We wanted Mom and Dad to be able to spot us in the crowd of people standing and waiting for the airplane to unload. Sometimes when I wait with the crowd at the airport, I like to pretend that I'm outside of the *Today Show* studios, hoping that I will be the one that Al Roker, the weatherman, notices and puts on television.

India made a sign that said WE MISSED YOU, MOM AND DAD. WHAT'D YA BRING ME? Then she wrote J/K at the bottom. She told me that J/K means "just kidding."

My sign said I LOVE YOU, MOM!!! I LOVE YOU, DAD!!! I LOVE YOU, STEWARDESS!!!

I wrote J/K after the word *stewardess*.

The manny wrote PLEASE DON'T HAVE ANY MORE CHILDREN! on his sign, with a big J/K at the bottom.

Belly didn't write anything. She stripped naked and painted herself blue and rolled across her sign. It looked like a big blue blob, but you could see the print of her bottom perfectly. She wrote J/K on hers, even though she didn't understand what it meant.

Lulu finished hanging her sign in the entryway and stepped back to congratulate herself. She was impressed, even though she had to spend twenty minutes painting red hearts over Belly's blue footprints that she had left when she walked across it.

"It looks great, Lulu," said the manny. I could tell she was annoyed that he didn't take her sign personally. The manny was carrying Belly, who was dressed in her prettiest pink dress and sparkling ruby red slippers, just like Dorothy's from *The Wizard of Oz*. She had been scrubbed clean, but there were still blue stains in the creases behind her knees.

The manny told me that I looked like a younger, shorter version of Ralph Lauren (India told me that Ralph Lauren was a polo player). I had used hair gel and was wearing my wedding blazer and my birthday bow tie with my blue jeans. India talked me out of wearing my sunglasses. She said it was overkill.

It was dark outside anyway.

We loaded into the Volkswagen Eurovan, and the manny drove us to the airport. The manny usually drives Belly to the Tomato Plant Preschool in the Volkswagen Eurovan. The door at her school says THE TOMATO PLANT PRESCHOOL—WHERE YOUR KIDS SPROUT AND GROW LIKE VINES. When I went to school there, we used to yell, "Where your kids shout and show their behinds." The teacher told us that it wasn't an appropriate thing to say. For three years after that I thought *behind* was a bad word. Whenever my dad would say, "Don't lag behind," I'd say, "Ummmm! You said a bad word."

Because we were all in the Volkswagen Eurovan, Belly thought that she was going to the Tomato Plant Preschool. She began to sing her going-to-school song that the manny had taught her. She sings it to the manny every day when they drive to school.

I'm going to school.
I'm going to school.
Where the kids are cool,
And the teachers drool.

Belly sang it once to her preschool teacher and classmates for show-and-tell. Her teacher, Miss Kim, didn't think it was as funny as Dad did when she called to tell him about it.

Lulu told me that she had devoted a whole four pages in "The Manny Files" to inappropriate things the manny had taught Belly. The going-to-school song was listed between "Throwing wet marshmallows at the ceiling" and "Singing opera songs in the mall."

We parked the car and raced down the long hallway of the airport. Inside the airport everybody was moving very quickly, the same way they do around someone who has a cold in the cold-medicine commercial. India read the blue monitor that looked like a television, and located the gate where Mom and Dad's plane would be arriving: B-7. Just as we found B-7, Lulu pointed at the plane that was pulling into the gate. I had the same feeling of excitement in my stomach that I get when *The Sound of Music* comes on television. Like I have to pee and throw up at the same time.

Strangers began walking out of the little door that delivered them off of the plane.

Grandmothers. Men in suits. Crying babies.

They all looked like they had been left in the dryer too long, with tired faces and wrinkled clothes.

I thought to myself, *Why don't any of these businessmen have no-iron shirts? They're so convenient.*

The man and woman standing next to us greeted their son wearing alien antennae on their heads. They held up a sign that said WELCOME BACK TO EARTH, SON. They told us that he had been in Los Angeles going to college.

I wish I had alien antennae on my head.

I heard Lulu squeal and saw her run into Dad's arms. He looked really tan. Belly ran to Mom, while India and I jumped up and down, holding our signs. The manny jumped with us.

People stared at him.

I waited until it was my turn to be hugged, which was usually after Belly.

I hugged Mom, who always smells like tea and sandalwood. I love that smell. I can always tell if she's been in a room, because the room smells like her.

I let go of Mom and shoved my way past Lulu, who was already telling Dad about the things the manny had done.

"Hey, kiddo," Dad said, with watery eyes and a sound in his voice like he needed to blow his nose. He hugged me and said, "Nice tie."

I thought, *If he likes the tie, just wait until he sees the feng shui coffee table.*

I've always wanted to make breakfast in bed for Mom on Mother's Day. Actually, I've always wanted to be served breakfast in bed on my birthday, but serving it to Mom would be almost as fun.

Lulu made a vase for Mom at pottery class. Lulu just started taking pottery class this week because she had Thursdays free. Her schedule after school is way busier than mine:

> Monday—Piano
> Tuesday—Origami
> Wednesday—Book club
> Thursday—Pottery
> Friday—Future Congressional
>   Leaders of America

My after-school schedule looks like this:

> Monday—
> Tuesday—

Wednesday—
Thursday—Take trash to curb
Friday—

India made certificates for Mom to use like money. They say "Redeemable only at Bank of India." Mom can give India a certificate anytime she wants, and India will do whatever the certificate says. Do the dishes. Give her a hug. Rotate the tires on the Eurovan.

I told India that she should make one that says "Drop Belly off at the orphanage."

She laughed, but she didn't make one.

Belly made something for Mom at the Tomato Plant Preschool. Her teacher, Miss Kim, had all of the children pour pink plaster of paris in a pie tin and then press their tiny handprint into it. Belly's handprint will complete Mom's set. We all made them when we were at the Tomato Plant Preschool. Lulu's has her name written on the back of hers in cursive. Lulu could write her name in cursive in preschool. Her hand was as big as mine is now. She gets mad when I show her that my hand fits perfectly in it.

India colored a rainbow in the middle of her handprint with markers. She also sprinkled glitter all over it so that it would sparkle.

Mine is just a plain handprint in pink plaster.

Lulu always points to it and says, "Look how little and cute his hand was."

I think she's just trying to get even with me because she has the same size hands as the Statue of Liberty.

Ms. Grant had our class plant seeds in Dixie cups to give to our mothers. I raised my hand and asked if I could plant mine in a fancy mint julep cup to make it more elegant.

Ms. Grant wouldn't let me.

We planted our seeds three weeks before Mother's Day so that they would be perfect little plants by the time we took them home. We watered them every day and measured their growth with a ruler. I tried to keep it a secret from Mom, but I couldn't hold it in. It was too exciting. I told her all about it and how I had even sneaked Miracle-Gro to school so that my seedling would grow to be the tallest one in class and maybe even in our school's history.

By the end of the first week Sarah's had sprouted and had three green leaves on its stem. Craig's cup had a little green seedling getting ready to explode through the dirt. He laughed at my Dixie cup. My seedling hadn't grown at all.

When Mom asked how my plant was growing, I lied and said, "It's so beautiful that Ms. Grant wants to keep it, but I won't let her because it's for you."

By the end of the second week Sarah's had a little bud that would soon be a flower. Craig's was three inches tall and had leaves. Mine was still just a cup of dirt. There was an ant crawling in it.

I said to Ms. Grant, "I'm not going to give my mom a Dixie cup full of dirt and ants for Mother's Day."

She said, "I don't understand what's happened. When Lulu was in my class, her plant ended up growing to be eight inches tall."

I thought to myself, *I'm surprised Lulu's big Amazon hands didn't squash the little seed.*

"I'm sure it will grow," said Ms. Grant. "Just be patient."

I went back to my desk and started being patient. I let the ant crawl all over my hand.

At home that afternoon Mom was watching the Weather Channel and ironing some of my shirts. She asked again how well the plant was growing.

But I changed the subject. I glanced at the Weather Channel and said, "Oh, good, rain in California. This should be an excellent year to buy California chardonnays." I had heard Uncle Max say this to Grandma once when the news showed mudslides in California. Grandma told him not to think about his palate when others were suffering.

Mom just looked at me and then went back to ironing.

When it was time to take our plants home for our mothers, I showed Ms. Grant that mine was just like me and hadn't grown an inch.

"That's so weird," was all she said. She didn't seem to care that all I had to give my mother for Mother's Day was a cup of dirt.

On the bus ride home India told me to tell Mom that she could use it as a mud mask to clean her face. I imagined Mom running and screaming through the house with mud and ants all over her face. I threw my stunted seedling in the trash can on my way off the bus.

"Bye, darlin'."

I just waved at the bus driver without looking at her.

I ran quickly through the kitchen so that Mom wouldn't notice that I didn't have a plant with me. She knew that today was the day we were bringing them home. She didn't even see me.

The manny was in the hallway putting the freshly washed towels in the closet. He knew something was wrong, so he wrapped a towel around me. It was just out of the dryer, so it was really warm.

"What's shakin', bacon?" the manny asked.

I started telling him the story without breaking up the sentences or stopping for a breath. "We were growing plants at school for our mothers, and mine didn't grow at all, and Ms. Grant didn't seem to care, she just told me to be patient, and I was, but it still didn't grow, and there was an ant in mine that I named Ferdinant, but he died, and now I don't have anything to give Mom for Mother's Day!"

"Whoa," the manny said. "You better take a breath before you lose consciousness."

I took a deep breath in and then let it out. "But what will I give her?"

"Give her something that you put a lot of thought into. What does your mother like to do on Mother's Day?"

"She likes to relax and sleep in," I said.

"How about sleeping pills?" said the manny.

I laughed and then thought about what Mom would like. "How about serving her breakfast in bed?" I looked at the manny.

"Brilliant!" he screamed, like I'd just discovered electricity. "You'll need the perfect serving tray," he said.

That's the thing about the manny. He really gets it.

We told Mom that we had "business to take

care of" and hopped right into the Eurovan. The manny said that this would be good practice for next year, when he was going to be Sarah Jessica Parker's personal shopper. I don't know who Sarah Jessica Parker is, but I guess she needs help carrying her shopping bags.

We drove to a store that was full of stationery, martini shakers, and books about throwing parties. There was one called *Be My Guest* that had beautiful table settings and overdressed people laughing as though the photographer had just said, "Pretend that somebody said something funny."

I want to go to a party like that.

The manny flipped through the book while I carefully tested each breakfast-in-bed tray. I tested for the perfect weight, beauty, and shine. The man at the shop was a friend of the manny's, so he showed me all the good deals. I chose a black lacquered tray with gold trim. It wasn't too heavy to carry, and it would hold a breakfast plate, a juice glass, and the morning paper.

"Excellent choice," said the manny's friend. "Donatella Versace was just in here and bought the same one for her mother."

I saw a picture of Donatella Versace in one of Mom's *Vogue* magazines. She pushes out her lips like she's getting ready to kiss somebody. I pushed my lips out the rest of the time I was in the shop.

The manny's friend wrapped the tray in beautiful silver wrapping paper and put a dark purple velvet ribbon around it. The manny said that it looked pretty enough to give to the queen of England.

I pulled my allowance money and some old candy wrappers out of my pocket to pay. The candy wrappers dropped on the floor, and I started to bend down to pick them up.

"Don't you dare," said the manny's friend. "Do you think that Donatella Versace picked up the candy wrappers that fell out of her pockets? It's my job to pick up after the important people who come into my shop."

I laughed, but when he wasn't looking, I picked up the candy wrappers and put them back in my pocket.

The manny bought something too, but he wouldn't tell me what it was. He said it was a surprise.

As we walked out of the store, I looked up at the manny. He had his lips pushed out too.

When we got home, Mom was putting away the ironing board. I sneaked around the back of the house and up into my room so that she wouldn't see. I hid Mom's present underneath my bed. I was hiding it from Mom and from Belly. Whenever Belly finds a wrapped present, she opens it. Last Christmas we left her alone in the living room for ten minutes one night, and she opened every single present under the Christmas tree. She came into the kitchen wearing a diamond bracelet that Dad had gotten for Mom.

After dinner that night the manny handed me a brown leather book wrapped in a white satin ribbon. I had picked it up and looked at it at the manny's friend's shop.

"It's a journal," said the manny. "You're supposed to write all your secret thoughts inside of it. It's sort of like Lulu's 'The Manny Files,' except nicer."

Lulu looked mortified and said, "I'll use it as evidence someday."

I thanked the manny for my journal and went to my room. The journal smelled like Dad's leather coat and felt expensive when I rubbed it against my cheek. The pages were blank and completely clean. They weren't white. They were that cream color that fancy stationery is made of.

On the first page I wrote:

> If you are reading this and your name is not
> Keats Rufus Dalinger, then may you suffer the
> guilt of knowing that you are reading somebody
> else's private thoughts. READ NO FURTHER
> UNLESS YOU ARE WILLING TO ADMIT THAT
> YOU HAVE A CRIMINAL MIND.

I turned the page and began my first entry into my journal.

May 11

Today during recess I went to my secret spot behind the Dumpster and started to cry. Nobody seemed to care that my plant hadn't grown at all. Ms. Grant even laughed with the rest of the class when Craig colored his thumb brown and said, "Hey, look, I'm Keats." I wasn't crying because of Craig. I was crying because Mom was expecting a plant that I had grown, and now she wasn't going to get one. When we had to line up to go back inside after recess, Sarah asked me if something was wrong. I told her that I thought I was getting a cold. She told me that our moms could share her plant. The manny told me that Sarah was very "thoughtful." I wrote her a note on

Mom's fancy stationery.

I'm excited for Mom to open her new breakfast-in-bed tray. I can't believe I cried over a Dixie-cup plant.

Born on this day: Martha Graham, Salvador Dalí, Irving Berlin

On Mother's Day, I woke up before Mom did and went downstairs to make her the surprise breakfast in bed. I'm not allowed to use the stove, so I served her a bowl of Cap'n Crunch, a side of string cheese, untoasted bread, and a glass of orange juice. I put a bright yellow daffodil in a little vase on the tray. Mom says daffodils are divine. I say the word *divine* when we eat out at fancy restaurants.

"How is your Roy Rogers?"

"Divine."

"How is your Shirley Temple?"

"Divine."

Mom sat with the tray on her lap and crunched on her cereal.

She loved her new tray. I could tell by the way she kept polishing it with her napkin. She opened her presents from Lulu, India, and Belly and stacked them on her new tray.

We all sprawled across Mom and Dad's bed

while they read the Sunday edition of the *New York Times*. Mom rubbed my back while she read the Arts and Leisure section.

I closed my eyes and wondered if Mom remembered that she was supposed to get a plant from me for Mother's Day.

Almost like I had thought it out loud, Mom said, "Those plants always die by Memorial Day anyway."

I guess moms do know everything.

When Mom was little, Uncle Max would tease her until she cried. He used to hide in the big heater vent and sinisterly bellow, "I'm coming for you," whenever she walked through the living room. She'd scream and cry and then go tell on him. Grandma would scream back, "You're both driving me insane." Uncle Max says that it was her favorite thing to say. I heard her say it once to him when she asked him what he wanted for Christmas and he told her, "Tattoos all the way up my arms."

Now Mom likes to scare us the way Uncle Max used to scare her. Sometimes she pretends to be a zombie, with her arms straight out in front of her and her eyes wide open but not blinking.

"Slowly I turn. Inch by inch. Step by step," she groans slowly, never turning her head or making sudden movements. When she does this, we squeal and laugh until eventually one of us hits our meltdown limit. That's what Mom calls it when laughter and fun are so overwhelming that they turn into terror and tears. I am usually the one to hit my meltdown limit first, even before Belly. It's embarrassing. I usually try to pretend that I'm having an allergy attack, but everybody knows that I'm crying.

With the house clean and the manny gone for the weekend (he said he wouldn't be back from the queen of England's country house until Monday), Mom decided it was a good day to stir all of us into a frenzy. When we asked her questions or spoke to her, she didn't respond. She just sat there like she was in a coma, only her eyes were open and she stared straight ahead with a blank expression.

She bugged out her eyes and taped her nose back like a pig nose with Scotch tape and chased us all over the house. Belly was slower, so Lulu and India took turns carrying her through the house and screaming. Up and down the steps. In and out of rooms. We screamed and screamed, but we were smiling. "Moooom," I whined with a little laugh, "stooop."

She cackled, "If I catch you, I'm going to put you in the attic." The attic has a big, old-fashioned door on it that creaks open to reveal steps that are much too steep to carry anything up. I went up there once with Dad. There are little board walkways that you have to stay on because if you step off of them and onto the pink insulation, you'll fall through the ceiling and into the room below. It happened to Grandma once at her house. She was putting away the Christmas lights and lost her balance and stepped into the insulation. Her legs went flying through the floor of the attic, which was the ceiling of the living room. Grandpa Pete was taking a nap in his easy chair when he was suddenly covered with white flakes of ceiling. He looked straight above him and saw Grandma's legs hanging and kicking from the ceiling. Mom says that Grandpa Pete didn't mind because Grandma had nice legs. Grandpa Pete died before I was born.

Anyway, Lulu, India, Belly, and I hid, perfectly quiet, underneath the bed.

I held my hand over Belly's mouth so that she wouldn't reveal our hiding spot. She slobbered all over my fingers. I wiped it on the carpet.

Lulu whispered, "India, stop tickling my feet with your toes."

"I'm not touching you, sweetie," said India.

India calls people sweetie when she has attitude. She says it like this: "sa-WHEAT-eeeee."

We looked down toward our feet and saw Mom tickling Lulu's toes. We screamed louder than before and barely escaped from underneath the bed. Mom even got one of Belly's socks off of her feet when she was grabbing at our legs.

Belly peed in her big-girl pants. Belly has just started to wear big-girl pants. Lulu claims that *she* was wearing big-girl pants when Mom and Dad brought her home from the hospital.

We ran down the hall, Belly with one sock on and a wet spot on the front of her sweatpants. We let out our breath and locked ourselves into the bathroom.

"Whew!" We all collapsed into the empty bathtub, which was cool and still had a few crunchy drying bubbles near the drain from the night before, when I'd washed my hair. I like washing my hair because afterward Mom dries it with the blow-dryer. She calls it styling.

Lulu said, "You know that she would never actually lock us in the attic if she caught us, because that would be child abuse and we'd sue her."

I got out of the tub and laid my head flat on the bathroom floor so that I could see through the thin slat underneath the door. There was a line of light with two dancing, shadowy socks.

India turned on the water to wash her hands, and I lifted my head up and said, "Shhh! She's on the other side of the door."

I put my head back down on the floor to take another look, shoving my eye as close to the door as I could to get a better view. There was Mom's eye staring right into mine.

"Ahhhhhhhh!" I screamed, very close to my meltdown limit.

"Ahhhhhhhh!" Belly screamed too.

We were all too scared to move. The only sound in the tiny porcelain room was our quick, thumping heartbeats trying to escape from our excited chests. We were prisoners trapped in our own bathroom, but instead of having striped uniforms and handcuffs, we had terry-cloth bathrobes and scented potpourri. Belly changed out of her sweatpants and into her tiny bathrobe with the hood that had mouse ears on it.

As we were lying there on the bathroom floor devising our escape plan, the telephone rang. Mom answered, and we could hear her talking. She didn't laugh like Woody Woodpecker and say, "You're kidding," like she usually does when she's on the telephone. We exploded out of the bathroom and quietly stood around her.

Mom said things like "Is she okay?" and "How bad is it?"

Lulu whispered, "Who is it?" and Mom shooed her away with her hand.

Mom hung up the telephone and sat down on

the couch. Belly, who still wanted to play, tugged at her pant legs. Mom sat just as she had before, like she was in a coma, but this time her face didn't seem blank.

I knew she wasn't playing.

India said, "Come on, I'll chase you." She started chasing Belly.

Mom called Dad at work and cried into the telephone.

She had hit her meltdown limit.

That night, after we were all supposed to be asleep, I could hear Dad's muffled voice on the other side of the wall. Usually Mom and Dad talk and laugh at night. Tonight they didn't laugh. They just talked.

I couldn't sleep, so I sneaked out of bed and tiptoed down the hall to India's room. The floor creaked, so I stopped in the hallway and looked at Mom and Dad's closed bedroom door. The light was shining from underneath it. The hairs on the back of my neck stood up. They always stand up when I'm afraid of getting caught out of bed after lights-out. Sometimes, after eleven thirty, I sneak through the dark house and down to the kitchen and have a glass of cranberry juice. Mom and Dad don't know.

I tiptoed faster when I reached India's room,

and finally ran for her bed. She was awake too.

"I can't sleep," I told her.

She said, "Maybe there's another jar of earwax underneath your bed."

"That's so funny I forgot to laugh," I said. Uncle Max slept over once, and I stayed up late with him. We watched old episodes of his favorite show, *Saturday Night Live*. There was a lady with frizzy hair who said, "That's so funny I forgot to laugh." I said it to Ms. Grant once, and she said I shouldn't be staying up so late.

She said it again when there was a knock at our classroom door.

"Who is it?" she said.

"Land shark," I said.

She glared at me.

She has no sense of humor.

I climbed into bed with India and felt her icy-cold toes touch mine.

"Who's sick?" I asked India. India always knows what's going on in our family. Mom and Dad talk to her like she's all grown up. Everyone talks to India like she's all grown up. At school one time India and I were walking down the hall together to catch the bus. Mr. Allen, our school principal, walked by going the other way and said, "Hey, India, thanks for your advice."

I looked at India, but she didn't look back at me. I still don't know what she advised him about, but it obviously wasn't about his toupee. He still wears that.

"Grandma fell and broke her hip," India said.

"Is she going to die?" I asked.

India said, "You don't die from a broken hip, silly."

But I think Sarah's grandma did.

"How did she break it?"

India leaned up on her elbow and adjusted her Snoopy pillow. I don't think that Mr. Allen would ask for her advice if he knew that she still slept on Snoopy sheets.

She began the story, "Grandma has been saving the money that she wins at canasta so that she can buy a water bed."

Canasta is a card game that Grandma plays every Tuesday with five other women as old as she is. Thelma, Wanda, Violet, Virginia, and June. I know their names because when Grandma hosts, I sometimes pretend to be their waiter and serve them cookies and lemonade. I decrumb the table between snacks. Thelma and Wanda are sisters who say mean things to each other and then laugh and hug. Violet always brings pie. Virginia talks like her throat hurts and has to go to the porch in between games to smoke cigarettes. She smells like the little glass room at the airport where people stand and smoke before they rush out to catch a plane with all the healthy people. June is my favorite. She is very fat, and her cheeks are pink. She always tips me.

India went on with the story.

"Grandma and June went to the Mattress King store to try out beds. Grandma lay down on one side of the bed and told June to lie on the other side. When June got on, the bed moved like a tidal wave. Grandma flew off of the bed and onto the floor. The store clerk said he tried to catch Grandma, but June says he really jumped out of the way of her flying body."

I felt badly because I wanted to giggle at the story.

India said, "Grandma's coming to live with us until her hip is better."

I crawled out of India's bed and tiptoed to the kitchen for a glass of cranberry juice and then back toward my bedroom. The door to Mom and Dad's room was open and the lights were off. I walked into their room and stood next to the bed. I stared at Mom's face without blinking until she finally startled awake. I always wake Mom up this way. Instead of shaking her or saying her name, I *will* her awake.

It always frightens her.

I said, "Grandma can sleep in my room when she comes to live with us."

She scooted over and let me crawl into the bed.

That night I slept in between Mom and Dad.

May 16

Craig and two of his friends started a club at school. They call it MASK, which stands for "Men Against Smelly Keats." Sarah said that I should tell Ms. Grant, but I think that would make them hate me even more than they already do. Sarah agreed and decided to start her own club. She calls it KICK, which stands for "Keats Is a Cool Kid." She wanted to have the first meeting, which would have been just the two of us, on the monkey bars during recess. I told her that I had to go to the bathroom, but I really went to my secret spot behind the Dumpster to cry. When we lined up to go inside, Sarah told me that her friends Sage, Caitlyn, Elizabeth, and Alexandra wanted to join KICK.

After school we visited Grandma in the hospital.

Mom and Dad asked if she would come live with us. Grandma said yes. The hospital smelled like an interstate rest area bathroom. I thought I was going to gag.

Dad asked how school was, and I told him about Sarah's club. I didn't tell him about Craig's club.

Born on this day: Liberace (it's not a cheese, like India said), Olga Korbut, Christian Lacroix

10 He Sounds Like a Butt Head

Grandma came to live with us the same day that my class took a field trip to the public swimming pool. That morning a shiny metal hospital bed was delivered into our living room. It definitely threw off the feng shui energy of the room. The same people who delivered the bed would be delivering Grandma later in the afternoon. The manny was helping Mom set up the living room like a bedroom for Grandma. That way she could watch television from her tall mechanical bed.

I kissed Mom and gave the manny a high five.

"Dude," said the manny, "don't forget your lunch."

I was going to be swimming all day, so the manny packed an aquatic-themed lunch: tuna sandwich, Swedish fish, Goldfish crackers. And a bag of sand.

I grabbed my lunch, backpack, swimsuit, and towel and ran for the bus.

The day before Ms. Grant had sat us all in a

circle and explained the rules of the swimming pool to us.

We already knew them.

No running.

No diving from the sides.

Swimsuits must be worn at all times.

That's the rule that Belly always breaks.

Ms. Grant looked at the boys and said, "Hey y'all, you need to be really organized tomorrow and keep your stuff together. I can't come into the boys' locker room to look for lost clothes." All the boys giggled at the thought of Ms. Grant in the boys' locker room.

The girls rolled their eyes at the boys.

We walked from the school over to the swimming pool in a single-file line from shortest to tallest. I was first in line. I'm always first in line. There were eight girls behind me before there was another boy.

It was Craig.

When I looked back at him, he said in a fake Texas accent, "Hey, Romeo, how you like all them girls?"

I could feel my cheeks go a dark shade of pink, and I turned around just in time to see that Ms. Grant had already started to walk toward the swimming pool. I ran to catch up. The person behind me ran to catch up with me.

And so on. We looked like an undulating cater-pillar shimmying down the sidewalk.

The pool was only a few blocks away, but the walk seemed endless. All the way there Ms. Grant asked me questions about how Lulu was doing. Soon Ms. Grant's questions about Lulu turned into Ms. Grant's stories about Lulu. The time Lulu brought the most canned goods for the food drive. The time Lulu made a model of a plant cell out of a cake mix and frosting. The time Lulu dressed up as Hillary Clinton for Halloween.

I wanted to tell Ms. Grant about the time Lulu cried when Mom told her that milk came from a cow's udder, but I didn't.

I was so relieved when we finally arrived at the swimming pool. We entered through the chain-link fence, and the girls went to the locker room on the left, and the boys to the right. The locker room smelled like Uncle Max's socks and chlorine. I opened up my bag and found my red swimsuit with a note from the manny pinned to it.

"Make a big splash," it said.

I remembered that I had worn my Scooby Doo underwear that day. So instead of stripping in the lockers with everyone else, I walked to the bathroom stall, closed the door, and changed in private. Once I was in my swimsuit, I carefully folded my clothes so that the Scooby Doo underwear was between my Hawaiian shirt and khaki pants. Nobody saw them. I put my folded clothes underneath one of the benches and walked out to the swimming pool with the rest of the boys.

Ms. Grant and Principal Allen split the kids up into groups based on swimming ability. They put me in the low group, which was mostly girls. There was one other boy named Scotty, but he had to wear floaties because one leg was shorter than the other. I pointed out to Mr. Allen that I knew how to swim and it was probably an oversight that I wasn't put in a more advanced group.

He looked down at me and said, "Why are you complaining? You could be back at the school doing math or English."

I wanted to grab the toupee off of his head, throw it in the middle of the swimming pool, and yell, "Rat in the pool. Rat in the pool."

But I didn't.

On my way back to my group I walked by Sarah. She was in the top group. Craig and the other boys, who look like they already have muscles, were in the top group.

Sarah saw my disappointment and said, "Swim with Scotty. He's nice."

He *is* nice.

Scotty and I made up a game. One of us would sit on the side of the pool and yell out a category (colors, states, Broadway plays), while the other one would jump in and try to name something from the category before he went underwater. It usually sounded like this: "Redblubblubblub." "Oklahoblubblub." "*The Lion Ki*blubblubblub."

Scotty's floaties helped him win the game.

When we opened our lunches, Scotty discovered that somebody had splashed water on his. His bagel looked like a sponge that was leaking cream cheese milk. I shared my lunch with him. He likes Swedish fish as much as I do. I ate the red ones. He ate the green ones. We built little sand castle pyramids out of the bag of sand until it had been an hour and the danger of cramping was gone.

When Ms. Grant blew the whistle to signal that the wait was over, I jumped in, grabbed my stomach, and pretended to have a cramp.

"If only I'd waited one more minute," I moaned, and pulled myself underwater.

Scotty laughed.

Sarah yelled from the high dive, "Judge me." She plummeted into the water headfirst.

"Ten," I yelled.

"Ten," Scotty yelled.

Sarah abandoned her group and spent the rest of the day swimming with Scotty and me.

At two thirty Ms. Grant blew the whistle and hollered. Ms. Grant doesn't yell. She hollers.

She hollered, "Go get dressed. We're fixin' to leave."

We climbed out and went into the locker rooms. Craig was the last one out of the pool. Ms. Grant had to yell at him twice. He bobbed up and down in the water and pretended that he couldn't hear her.

I grabbed my folded clothes from underneath the bench and went into the bathroom stall to change. I unfolded my shirt and pants but couldn't find my underwear. I shook out my Hawaiian shirt and khaki pants and even rifled through the pockets. Nothing. I looked inside my shoes, in case I was suffering from a brain lapse and had maybe stuffed them in there.

They were nowhere to be found.

I walked back out into the lockers to see if I had dropped them, but they weren't on the floor. Where could they be? I felt like Mom searching for her car keys (she found them in the refrigerator once).

I raced back to the bathroom stall and decided to get dressed without them. Uncle Max calls going without underwear "going commando."

When he says this, Lulu pretends to dry heave.

I got dressed, minus my underwear, and exited the locker room with the rest of the boys.

We lined up in single file, again shortest to tallest, and began walking back to our school. I could feel my khaki pants right up against my skin. I turned around to see where Scotty was in line but instead saw Craig walking along with my Scooby Doo underwear on the top of his head like a hat. Nobody would have known that they were mine if Mom hadn't written my name on the waistband.

KEATS, in big black letters, stretched across Craig's forehead.

What a crummy day. I even had to ride the bus home alone because Lulu had to go to piano lessons and India had an after-school project. As the bus pulled away, I saw Craig standing on the sidewalk in front of the school whipping my underwear around in circles above his head and waving to me with his other hand.

I wanted the bus to get me home as fast as it could because I thought I might burst into tears at any minute. But then I remembered that Grandma was going to be there when I got home. I didn't want to cry then. I couldn't wait to see her.

When the bus reached my stop, I leaped out the door to race home.

"See you tomorrow, darlin'." I barely heard the bus driver.

Housman met me in the driveway and ran with me into the house.

My hair was still wet from swimming when I spotted Grandma. She was lying up on her throne bed in the middle of the living room. She told me later that it was more comfortable than the water bed. Belly was taking a nap on pillows on the floor next to Grandma's bed.

And Uncle Max was there! He and the manny were laughing in the kitchen. They didn't stop smiling as they talked to each other. They looked like the hosts of the morning show on television. It was like they'd known each other forever.

I ran and jumped into Uncle Max's arms. Housman jumped up and down at Uncle Max's feet.

Uncle Max groaned and pretended to have a bad back when he picked me up.

He said, "Keats, you've grown so much. Is that a mustache?" He looked closely at my upper lip.

Uncle Max had been in San Francisco for three months going to museums and meeting with art gallery owners. He brought Lulu, India, Belly, and me kimonos from a little Japanese shop in San Francisco. Mine was red. He brings us the best presents from his trips.

I put the red kimono on over my clothes, sucked my cheeks in, and walked through the kitchen like a fashion model. Uncle Max and the manny were still laughing when I went to check on Grandma.

I gave Grandma a hug, and she asked me how school was. I didn't tell her about Craig and my underwear because I thought it seemed silly compared with her broken hip. I did tell her about Scotty and how Sarah swam with us and about the game we made up.

She said, "Keats, my feet are cold. Could you please rub them for me?"

I went to the end of the bed and began rubbing Grandma's feet. They *were* cold. Mom's feet are always cold too. She says that bad circulation runs in her family. I thought about Grandma's feet hanging through the ceiling over Grandpa Pete's head.

She fell asleep.

"Come back at about six thirty," I heard the manny tell Uncle Max before the door shut.

The manny turned to me and said, "Did Ms. Grant look babe-alicious in her swimming suit?"

I smiled but didn't laugh.

"What's wrong?" asked the manny. "Did you forget that I'm hilarious?"

So I told him about being put in the low

swimming group, and about Craig and his new hat, which happened to be my underwear.

"He sounds like a butt head," the manny said, laughing at his own joke.

It took me a minute to laugh, but when I did, the manny said, "Oh, thank goodness, I thought I'd lost my gift of humor. I don't think I could cope with losing my humor and my hair all in one lifetime."

I laughed again.

Then the manny told me that Craig probably did that to be the center of attention. He said that Craig probably knows that I don't have to do anything to be the center of attention because I have natural charisma and style. He said that I'm just like John F. Kennedy, and Craig is more like Richard Nixon.

I saw a television show about Richard Nixon on the Biography Channel. He had cheeks like Droopy Dog.

"Go get your homework done," said the manny. "Your uncle Max is coming to dinner tonight."

I disappeared to my room and didn't come out again until I was called for dinner. I had been putting all of my sweaters and winter things into big Rubbermaid tubs, replacing them with khaki shorts, Hawaiian shirts, and linen pants that Dad had brought for me from Mexico.

When I walked through the living room, Grandma's bed was empty and her wheelchair was gone. She was in the dining room with everyone else. They screamed, *"Surprise!!!"* when I walked in. Everybody was sitting around the dining-room table. Grandma was wheeled up next to Lulu.

They all had underwear on their heads.

Even Lulu, who hates the word *underwear.*

Mom had on a pair of Dad's boxers.

Dad had one of Mom's bras.

Lulu had a pair of India's flowered panties.

India had Lulu's Tuesday underwear.

Belly had DecapiTina's little white ones hanging off one ear.

Grandma had on one of Belly's nighttime pull-up diapers.

The manny had a pair of boxer briefs.

And Uncle Max was wearing a pair of Grandma's big lacy ones, the ones that my sisters had held up and laughed at when they unpacked Grandma's suitcase.

The manny handed me a pair of my own Scooby Doo underwear to wear on my head.

We ate the entire dinner that way. Dad even answered the door with Mom's bra on his head.

It was Lucy, our next-door neighbor, selling Girl Scout Cookies.

He bought four boxes of Thin Mints.

May 22

Scotty joined Sarah's KICK club today. When he saw my Scooby Doo underwear on Craig's head, he pulled down the waistband of his jeans to show me that he had the same pair of Scooby Doo underwear on, only with a blue waistband instead of red.

I found Lulu's "The Manny Files" today. She was at Margo's house working on a school project, and she had accidentally left it on the dining-room table. I opened it and started to read the first page, but I slammed it closed when the manny walked into the room. He asked me how I'd feel if Lulu found my journal and read *my* secret thoughts. I didn't see anything in her notebook except the words "belongs in a circus." I think the manny belongs in a circus too, but probably for different reasons than Lulu does.

Born on this day: Sir Laurence Olivier, Mary Cassatt, Harvey Milk

11 Which Do You Like Better, Bert or Ernie?

Our last writing assignment for the school year was to write a one-paragraph essay about what we want to be when we grow up. Sarah wants to be a horse veterinarian. Scotty wants to be a children's doctor. The poofy-red-haired girl wants to own a beauty salon. Craig wants to play on a professional football team.

I think that Craig should be more realistic. Maybe he'll get to play in a prison league someday.

I want to be a concierge in a fancy hotel like the Ritz-Carlton or the Four Seasons. The concierge gets to wear a suit and make reservations at five-star restaurants and theater shows for people who have forgotten how to do it themselves. Last year, before Grandma fell and broke her hip, India and I went to New York City with her. We stayed at the Waldorf-Astoria and she took us out to a fancy dinner. Lulu was at a sleepover and Belly stayed home with

Mom and Dad because she was too little.

Grandma asked the concierge, "Could you recommend a nice restaurant that has wonderful food and elegant ambience? Oh, and we'd prefer a place where the maître d' doesn't kick the children when nobody's looking."

The concierge had short black hair that looked wet and shiny. His knuckles were hairy. He looked like one of the male models from Mom's *Vogue* magazines. He wore round silver cuff links.

He leaned in toward us and said, "Nobu has a fabulous young chef, and the soft-shell crab rolls are divine."

My ears tickled when he said the word *divine*.

"Balthazar is also quite fancy, and the food is sublime."

The back of my neck tingled when he said the word *sublime*.

Grandma told the concierge to make a reservation for four at Balthazar for seven thirty, and she slipped him five dollars with a handshake. India didn't even notice.

"Who else is coming to dinner?" I asked Grandma as we rode the elevator up to our room.

"It's a surprise," she said back to me.

Back in the hotel room I wore the complimentary shower cap and took a bath. I changed my clothes four times before India finally yelled, "Keats! We have to go!"

We arrived at the restaurant five minutes before our seven thirty reservation. I had on my wedding suit and bow tie. India wore a red silky skirt and white collared shirt, the same kind Dad wears to work. She had it tied at the waist, with the knot on her hip. Around her neck she wore the little string of pearls that Grandma had given to her last Christmas. Grandma wore a black velvet shawl over white pants and a white turtleneck. She looked divine and sublime.

I stood and watched the people having dinner at their tables. Everybody wore black. They looked like they were having a wonderful time. Clanking wineglasses. Laughing. Giving cheek kisses to one another when they said hello.

I can't wait to grow up.

Whenever the front door opened, I would look over to see if it was our surprise dinner guest. I thought that it might be Andy Warhol or Liza Minnelli. They're the two most famous people in New York City. Andy Warhol is a skinny artist who wears a white wig and paints portraits of movie stars. Liza Minnelli sings just like her

mom, who was Dorothy in *The Wizard of Oz*.
Whenever I read anything about New York City,
Andy Warhol's and Liza Minnelli's names are
mentioned. India told me that Andy Warhol
wasn't alive anymore and that Liza Minnelli
probably had a personal chef and didn't go out
to eat. I still kept an eye on the door and hoped.

When the door swung open, it was better
than Andy Warhol and Liza Minnelli. It was
Uncle Max, dressed from head to toe in black,
except for a white scarf around his neck. He
looked just like Halston, the clothing designer.
Halston is always in the pictures with Andy
Warhol and Liza Minnelli. Uncle Max gave India
and me high fives and then hugged Grandma.

Grandma asked the maître d' if he could sit
us by a table that was having an interesting
conversation, because she wanted to eavesdrop.

"I'll do my best," said the grinning maître d',
who winked at Uncle Max.

We sat next to a table full of businessmen
who were talking about the last stock reports
and the effectiveness of casual Fridays.

Grandma pretended to cover a yawn like she
was bored.

Dinner at Balthazar was fantastical. Sarah
would be so jealous.

I ordered lobster macaroni and cheese and a Roy Rogers. India ordered sea bass, wasabi mashed potatoes, and a ginger ale and cranberry juice. We shared our plates.

Uncle Max ordered coq au vin, which he told me was chicken in wine sauce. He shared his plate with India and me.

Grandma liked her meat loaf so much that she didn't share with anybody.

She did share her bottle of wine with Uncle Max. It was a fancy bottle. I could tell because there were Italian words on it. I took the cork home and put it on my windowsill.

I wrote a note to Uncle Max on a little piece of paper: "Which wine do you like better, red or white? Circle one."

He circled *red*.

He wrote back on the bottom of the note: "Which do you like better, Bert or Ernie? Circle one."

I didn't circle either. Instead I wrote, "Grover."

When the bill came, Uncle Max pulled out a silver money clip that had twenty-dollar bills folded neatly inside of it. I'm going to ask for a silver money clip for my next birthday. Grandma insisted that he put his money away. She paid for all of us with her American Express SkyMiles card. She said she needed a vacation anyway.

After dinner we went to a play called *Kiss Me, Kate*. It was very funny. India said it was based on William Shakespeare's play called *The Tying of My Shoe*. I looked at all of the actors' feet, and nobody even had shoelaces.

At the play I sat in between Grandma and Uncle Max. India sat on the other side of Grandma. Uncle Max and Grandma kept looking at each other and laughing. I kept watching them so that I knew when to laugh.

After the play we said good-bye to Uncle Max, and Grandma took us back to the Waldorf-Astoria. The concierge was still behind his desk.

I went over to him and said, "My lobster macaroni and cheese was sublime, and my Roy Rogers was divine. Thank you for the fabulous recommendation."

I shook his hand and slipped him a one-dollar bill just like Grandma had done.

He smiled and said, "You're too kind, sir."

Grandma grabbed my hand, and with India on the other side of her, we walked through the lobby to the elevator.

I got an A on my "What I Want to Be When I Grow Up" paper.

Ms. Grant wrote, "Interesting choice," in red marker at the top of the paper.

I smiled and remembered my coconut.

BE INTERESTING.

May 26

I got an A on my writing assignment. Ms. Grant read it to the class. Scotty told me that it was very good and that my grandma sounded classic. Scotty says everything that he likes is "classic." Sarah asked me for a copy for her mom to read. When I raised my hand to be excused to go to the bathroom, Craig raised his hand and asked if he could go get a drink of water. Ms. Grant let us both go. I tried walking fast in front of Craig, but he walked just as fast and kept kicking the back of my heel. He said, "You may be smart, but don't forget you're smelly. And nobody likes a smelly person." I didn't say anything. I just hoped that he would go to the water fountain when I went into the bathroom. He didn't. He followed me into the bathroom, and I could feel him staring at the back of my head while I peed in the urinal. When I washed my hands, he turned on the sink next to me and splashed water on the front of my jeans. I ran out of the bathroom and down the hall to my classroom. Craig followed me.

When we walked through the door, Craig pointed to the front of my pants and said, "Ms. Grant, I don't think Keats made it to the bathroom." I told Ms. Grant that I had accidentally spilled on myself when I was washing my hands. Craig looked at me like he couldn't believe that I didn't tell on him. He didn't say anything else about it.

At recess I went behind the Dumpster and cried. I guess Craig had seen me go behind there, because he followed me. He ran to Ms. Grant, yelling, "Ms. Grant, Ms. Grant, Keats is crying behind the Dumpster." He didn't care that I was crying, he just wanted all the other kids to know. I told Ms. Grant that I had a stomachache. She called my mom, and the manny came to pick me up. Ms. Grant told him how good she thought my essay was.

I told the manny what Craig had done to me and that I couldn't wait to be grown up. The manny told me that there were always going to be people in the world who acted like that, no matter how old I got. He said that the most important thing was to realize that those people might have unhappy things in their lives and their only way to handle them was to try to make other people unhappy too.

I asked him what he would have done, and he said he would have laughed and told Ms. Grant that if there were more of a budget for the educational system, he wouldn't have to use the front of his jeans to dry off his hands.

I love the manny.

Born on this day: Dr. Sally Ride, Stevie Nicks, John Wayne

Grandma likes the manny as much as I do. They play cards, tell each other stories, and listen to opera music together. Their favorite opera is called *La Bohème,* by someone named Puccini, who was born almost 150 years ago. Dad says that Puccini had the same birthday as Mom— December 23.

La Bohème is about a girl named Mimi and a boy named Rodolfo who have no money but fall in love on Christmas Eve. Dad says that in the end Mimi gets sick and dies, but that it's okay because she spent her last days with someone who loved her.

One night after dinner Uncle Max and Dad did the dishes so that the manny and Grandma could prepare for their after-dinner surprise performance. I can't figure out if Uncle Max is visiting us more because of Grandma or because he's friends with the manny. I don't really care. I'm just glad that he comes over.

Grandma and the manny's surprise after-dinner performance was a lip sync to one of Puccini's opera songs. India did a choreographed dance in front of them. Grandma charged us each a dollar to see the show. She put the money in the canasta-winnings jar that she keeps underneath her bed. Even though she's living in our house, she still hosts canasta games on Tuesdays when she's feeling well enough. The manny plays too. He always loses. Most of the money in the jar used to be his.

India called us into the living room.

We filed in from the dinner table and sat on the couch facing Grandma's bed. I sat on Uncle Max's lap. My red sheets were hanging from the ceiling like a theater curtain in front of Grandma's big metal hospital bed.

The curtain opened and we all clapped really loudly. Belly put one of her fists in the air and went, "Woof, woof, woof." We don't know where she learned that. Lulu said that the manny probably taught her. She quickly glanced at Mom, hoping that she would realize how inappropriate the manny was. Mom just smiled.

Grandma was lying in her bed and had on a tall, gray-haired wig with white makeup and bloodred lipstick. There was a mole drawn above her lip, and her bed was draped with dark purple velvet.

She looked like George Washington if he'd been Georgette Washington.

India had on a black leotard and tights.

The manny was wearing a tuxedo. The manny says that it's important to have a tuxedo in your closet because you never know when you might be invited to tea with the queen or to the Oscars.

(Note to self: Get tuxedo measurements.)

When our applause died down, the manny spread out his arms and said, "Thank you, fine patrons of the arts. Please turn off your cellular telephones and refrain from using flash photography during the performance."

Dad pulled his cell phone out of his pocket and switched it off.

Uncle Max had those little opera binoculars. He held them up to his face.

The manny went on, "Singing the part of Mimi will be the unbearable diva *Grandma*ria Callas. Playing Rodolfo will be the stunningly handsome Luciano Mannyrotti, and providing movement in the form of dance will be, straight from Cirque du Fourth Grade, India Dalinger."

We clapped with the tips of our fingers. The kind of clap that doesn't make any noise and requires good posture. Lulu leaned over to my ear and said that she was clapping for Grandma and not for the manny. She didn't even whisper it. I looked up at the manny and could tell by his eyes that he had heard Lulu. When he saw that I was watching him, he smiled, but I think Lulu had hurt his feelings.

India pushed Play on the CD player and the music began. Grandma started lip-syncing the opera. You could tell that she didn't really know the words. She was just moving her mouth like this: *Waaaaaa wa wa wa wa waaaa.*

Grandma sang the woman's part. The manny sang the man's part, and India danced tragically in front of them. She held her chest a lot and looked like she was in pain. The same way she did when I accidentally killed all of her sea monkeys by feeding them garlic. Lulu had told me that sea monkeys were really brine shrimp, and I love garlic shrimp at the fancy restaurant.

At the end of the song Grandma and the manny had their arms stretched out as long as they would go and their mouths open wide like they were getting a dental checkup. India was a dead butterfly on the floor.

We clapped again. Only this time we stood up.

Uncle Max threw radishes on the stage. He said that radishes were the closest thing to roses that we had. Grandma started eating one.

The manny opened and closed the curtain several times, and everybody gave a solo bow. Even Belly, who wasn't even in the performance.

Grandma and the manny are always doing things like this. Uncle Max says that they should go on the road or open up a show in Las Vegas and call themselves Granny and the Manny.

When Grandma watches her soap operas, the manny dresses her up as a different character each day. She doesn't care what soap opera she watches, because she thinks that they are all the same anyway. Grandma always pretends to be the character that she is dressed like. The evil stepsister, Tracy. The misunderstood doormat, Jan, who is now in a coma. The conniving Lisa, who has been married to everybody on the show and has already died twice.

One time when we got home from school, Grandma was dressed in a dark red wig and had on a lot of eye makeup and lipstick. She had a big fake jewel necklace around her neck and was screaming at the manny with a fake accent.

"I know that it was you who ran off to Bolivia with my daughter and brainwashed her. I had to bury seven husbands to get this rich, and I'm not about to hand it over to you without a fight."

The manny whispered back just loud enough

for us to hear, "Ah, Lisa, you are right not to trust me, but you are too late. I put rat poison in your martini."

Grandma pretended to choke and clasped on to her throat.

"You horrible, horrible manny." She keeled over with her eyes open and hung her tongue out of the side of her mouth.

Lulu rolled her eyes and huffed, "Don't *ever* do that in front of my friends."

India and I cheered the performance, and Grandma lifted her head and nodded a bow to us. Then she pretended to die again.

We ran over to give her a hug, and she said, "Always remember, kids, head and shoulders, knees and toes."

Then she drifted off to sleep with the red wig crooked on her head and her lipstick smeared across her face.

Grandma says funny things after she takes her pills. One time when I was rubbing her feet, she said that she wanted me to pull her toes off because she would like to be a toe donor. She and the manny had watched a television program about organ donors. She told the manny that she had marked on her driver's license that she wanted to donate her organs.

She said, "Pull them off, Keats. There are all

those unfortunate, toeless people who are waiting on donors for transplants. I don't need mine anymore."

I pulled on her toes.

The manny brought in a plastic cup full of baby carrots and shook them.

"Okay, Keats pulled them all off. We'll just be taking these to the hospital," said the manny.

"Thank you, Keats," said Grandma. "I hope this makes lots of other families happy." She drifted off to sleep like she always does after she says something silly.

The manny and I looked at each other and giggled.

May 29

Mom told me that Grandma's feet are cold because she doesn't get enough blood circulated to them. She said that it's important that Grandma moves her feet every once in a while, or her feet will get numb and it will hurt for her to walk.

I stopped making eye contact with Craig at school because when I do, he makes the same throat-slicing hand sign that Lulu makes about the manny. The manny told me that next year he wants to be a trapeze artist for Cirque du Soleil, even though he's never been on a trapeze. The manny thinks about next year a lot. I think Lulu is making him want to leave earlier than he planned. I told Mom that I hated Lulu because she was mean to the manny. Mom got mad at me. She told me that *hate* was too strong of a word, and I should never use it unless I was talking about lima beans. She told me that it was okay to say that Lulu bugged me. LULU BUGS ME.

Born on this day: John F. Kennedy, Bob Hope, T. H. White

My birthday is in June, the week after school is out for summer vacation. I usually have my school birthday party the week before my actual birthday. I like it that way because it makes my birthday a weeklong event. Uncle Max always calls that week Keatstock. He says that when he was about my age, there was a concert that lasted for three days. It was called Woodstock, and everybody listened to music, climbed scaffolds, and rolled in the mud.

On my birthday last year Uncle Max and I rolled in the mud.

This year my birthday is on the last day of school. Ms. Grant said that I could bring cupcakes or cookies to celebrate. Everybody brings cupcakes or cookies. I wanted to bring something original.

Like wedding mints. Or mocha lattes. Or kebobs.

I finally decided on Dutch babies, which are kind of like crepes but have more powdered sugar.

We usually have Dutch babies for breakfast, but this year they would be the perfect birthday treat to set the standard for all of next year's parties.

The morning of the last day of school and, most important, of my party, the manny helped me mix flour, eggs, milk, and sugar into a bowl and then fry them in a pan like large pancakes. The manny sang, "Yes, sir, that's Dutch baby. No, sir, don't mean maybe," while he collected the powdered sugar, lemons, and strawberries to take to school.

The manny drove me to school because I had too much stuff to carry on the bus and Mom was afraid that I would drop the Dutch babies on the floor of the school bus and they would be trampled.

I said, "Trampled babies would probably make the front page of the newspaper."

The manny laughed at my joke.

Mom rolled her eyes the same way that Lulu does.

I told Ms. Grant that my party treat would be appropriate for a first-thing-in-the-morning party. She smiled when I said the word *appropriate*. I think that won her over, because she held up her hands and said, "Quiet, y'all, Keats is fixin' to hand out a birthday surprise. Let's sing 'Happy Birthday' to him."

I think the manny won her over too. When

we walked in, he said, "Wow, Keats, she's even prettier than you said." I looked over at Craig to make sure that he didn't hear what the manny had said. Craig didn't hear. He was searching through his messy desk for a pencil.

Ms. Grant flipped her hair like she was one of Charlie's Angels and asked the manny if he wanted to stay and help with the party. The manny sat in a desk that was way too small for him. It was one of those desks that had the chair attached to it, so he couldn't scoot the chair out. He squeezed lemons on the Dutch babies and covered them with powdered sugar and strawberries while the kids sang to me.

"Happy birthday to you,
Cha-cha-cha,
Happy birthday to you,
Cha-cha-cha,
Happy birthday, dear Keats,
Happy birthday to you,
Cha-cha-cha."

Then Sarah sang, "And many more on channel four, Scooby Doo on channel two, naked lady on channel eighty."

Everybody laughed. Ms. Grant wasn't going to until she saw the manny laughing.

Then Scotty sang, "This is your birthday song, it isn't very long, *hey*!"

"All right, y'all, that's enough," said Ms. Grant. "Remember, nobody gets to take a bite until the birthday boy takes one first. Keats, do you want to have your friend help you?"

She pointed to the manny.

The manny stood up and started walking with the whole desk and chair attached to his bottom.

The kids all laughed.

"Ha, ha, ha, ha, ha."

He removed the desk and followed me, holding the plate while I passed out Dutch babies to my classmates.

"What are those?" asked Craig.

"Dutch babies," I said.

"Oooh! I'm not eating any babies," said Craig.

The manny said, "Don't worry. There aren't any bones, and we removed the eyes."

The kids all laughed again, and I put a Dutch baby on Craig's napkin.

When I was just about finished passing out the treats, I looked over at Craig. He had powdered sugar on his lips and he was leaned over so that his elbow covered his Dutch baby. He looked like he'd been kissing the chalkboard.

I didn't even care that he hadn't waited for me to have the first bite.

He liked them and I knew it.

The manny gave me a high five and said, "I'll be back to pick up you, Lulu, and India after school."

He even gave Ms. Grant a high five and said, "Catch you on the down low."

All the kids laughed. Even Craig.

We spent the rest of the day spraying cleaner on our desks and organizing Ms. Grant's storage closet. There was a whole shelf full of Lulu's old projects. I accidentally stepped on one when it fell on the floor. I "accidentally" threw it in the trash, too.

When the bell was about to ring, you could hear every classroom in the building counting down.

"Five, four, three, two, one. Wooohoooo!"

It was so loud that Ms. Grant had to cover her ears. Ms. Grant doesn't like it when people are loud. At an assembly once I was talking when I wasn't supposed to be. I was sitting by Sarah and asked her where her mother got her Tabu perfume, because I wanted to get some for Grandma.

"Shhhhhh!" Ms. Grant said.

She did it so loud I thought she was going to start flying around the room like a balloon does when it isn't tied in a knot and you let go of it.

It made me laugh out loud to think of Ms. Grant flying around the auditorium.

I had to stay after class and clean the Lulu shelf in the closet.

Today Ms. Grant didn't make anybody stay after school. In fact, she ran faster than I've ever seen her move to get to the classroom door. She stood there and said good-bye to each of us as we left, like she was an airline stewardess and we had all been guests on a yearlong flight. I gathered my things and said good-bye to Ms. Grant, and then I raced to meet India at her classroom. We walked out of the school until next fall.

The manny was parked right in front of the school. He had a long black wig on his head and black circles painted under his eyes. He kept sticking his tongue out. The Volkswagen Eurovan had a song blasting out of it.

"School's out for summer.
School's out forever."

The manny said that the song was by Alice Cooper, a famous rock star from the seventies who dressed in tight clothes and looked like he never slept.

I've never heard of a boy named Alice, but he

sounds like a vampire and he screams more than he sings.

When we climbed into the van, Lulu was already inside lying flat on the floor.

"Close the door before anybody sees me!" she screeched in horror.

HAPPY BIRTHDAY, KEATS was written all over the windows in shoe polish, and there were cans hanging off the back like somebody had just gotten married. Kids stopped to read the windows.

"What's up, homeslice?" the manny asked, and handed me a pair of sunglasses to put on. He handed India a pair too.

We drove away from the school.

Everybody waved to us.

14 You're Starting to Look Old

I ran into the house to tell Mom and Dad that the Dutch babies were a big hit and that next year I wanted to take foie gras and toast tips. Foie gras is duck liver. My dad bet me five dollars that I wouldn't eat it, so I did. I liked it. It tasted like buttery, mushy bologna. I had foie gras at the fancy restaurant where the guy who seats you looks you up and down when you walk in. He starts with your shoes, then slowly scans up to the top of your head and then back down to your shoes again.

I always wear my bow tie.

I think that's why we always get a good table.

As soon as I reached the living room, Grandma yelled out, "Bon voyage!"

She must have just taken her pills.

The living room was draped from floor to ceiling in red streamers and balloons, with a WELCOME TO KEATSTOCK, DON'T EAT THE GREEN M&M'S sign taped to the wall. It looked like the stage of the Democratic National Convention when the presidential candidate is announced. I saw it on television last year. A man wearing a dark suit and blue tie danced like Frankenstein to "We are family, I got all my sisters with me." His wife, who wore a red dress and looked like someone in a teeth-whitening commercial, danced and waved to the audience while she swung her daughter's arms in the air. India said that this was why politics and entertainment should never mix.

Grandma's bed was covered with balloons and streamers. She looked like she was riding on a Macy's Thanksgiving Day Parade float. She even waved with an elbow, elbow, wrist, wrist. The same way the Rockettes do it in the parade. Whenever the Rockettes come on in the parade, Mom, Dad, India, and Uncle Max join arms and kick their legs in unison in front of the television.

Uncle Max can kick pretty high. One time he kicked a lamp off of Mom's desk. I would've grounded him, but Mom just laughed.

I got to choose what we had for dinner that night. Fish sticks, mashed potatoes, and spinach. I've liked spinach ever since I saw Popeye eat it on television when I was two years old. I used to sing, "I'm Popeye the sailor man, I live in a garbage can, I love to go swimmin' with bald-headed women, I'm Popeye the sailor man. Toot, toot."

I just learned last year that I have been singing it all wrong.

After dinner Mom brought in a cherry cheesecake with nine candles on it. Cherry cheesecake is my favorite. Grandma used to make it for me, but this year she gave Mom her recipe so that she could make it.

I blew out the candles and made a secret wish.

Everybody cheered, and I started to open my presents. The first present was from Mom and Dad. It was a clothes valet. It was made of oak and had a place to hang your shirt and jacket and your pants, and even a wooden dish on top to keep cuff links, watches, and pocket change in.

Mom and Dad got me a clothes valet because every night before school, I lay out my clothes. I pick out underwear, socks, shoes, pants, a shirt, and a sweater and lay them in the middle of my room. Every time Dad walks by my room, he's startled because my clothes are lying in the middle of my floor like a body, only flat on the floor, like a body doing the yoga corpse position. We did yoga last spring in PE. I was the only one who could do the tree position. The next week we played basketball. I scored a basket, but it was accidentally for the other team. Everyone forgot how good I was at yoga.

Dad said, "Now you can hang your clothes up and I won't call 911 every time I walk by your room."

He's so dramatic. I heard Mom call him dramatic once.

Lulu, India, and Belly gave me a grown-up watch with a black leather braided band. Instead of numbers the face of the watch had Roman numerals. I didn't know how to read it, so when anybody asked me what time it was, I'd write it down on paper. "I:VI" meant one thirty. "VII:IV" meant seven twenty. "XX till X" meant twenty till ten.

I kept the watch in the wooden bowl on top of my clothes valet.

Uncle Max had wrapped up one of his paintings for me to have. It was bigger than our television. He had used thick black paint as a background and had painted two angel wings on it. The wings had some real white feathers glued into them. His card said, "Use your wings to fly away, then use them again to come back."

I opened Grandma's gift next. It was her canasta jar full of dollar bills.

Grandma's pills kicked in: "I thought you could use the money to buy some car insurance."

I counted it later. There were twenty-seven one-dollar bills in it. A few weeks later I asked the manny to take me to Saks Fifth Avenue to spend my new money. I bought a pair of red cashmere socks. I thought the money would have gone further than that. The manny pulled out his American Express and bought a matching pair of socks for himself and a pair for Grandma's cold feet.

"Plastic goes a lot further than cash," he said, signing his receipt.

The last gift that I opened was wrapped in bright red wrapping paper and was tied in white ribbon. The card said, "To: Keats. You're starting to look old. I love you. The manny."

I tore off the wrapping paper and saw a red Saks Fifth Avenue box. I carefully opened the box because I wanted to save it to keep pictures in.

Inside the box was a silver money clip with my initials engraved on it.

"That's so your money doesn't get mixed up with your pocket trash," said the manny, smiling.

I hugged and kissed everyone and thanked them for the gifts. Uncle Max and the manny left in the same car. They were going to a late movie.

The manny said, "See ya round town, clown," and they left.

I ran to my room and hung my clothes for the

next day on my new valet. I put the cards from Uncle Max and the manny in the Saks Fifth Avenue box and put it in the top drawer of my dresser. I took out the dollar bills from the jar of money that Grandma had given me. I folded them neatly and placed them in the silver money clip.

At bedtime I turned out all the lights in my room except for the reading lamp by my bed.

I began to write in my journal.

June 1

I had the best birthday. Sarah told me that there are ten people in her Keats Is a Cool Kid club. Craig told me that he thought he had food poisoning from my Dutch babies. Scotty said it was probably from chewing on his dirty fingernails. During our last recess of the school year I went to my secret crying spot behind the Dumpster. I didn't cry. Instead I wrote my name with a pen on the edge at the bottom of the Dumpster.

Tonight when I blew out the candles, I wished that the manny could be part of my family forever, like Uncle Max.

Born on this day: Keats Dalinger

15 I'm Melting, I'm Melting

The summer light shines through the window and in on Grandma every evening. It reflects off her metal bed and makes little dancing lights across the ceiling. The sun makes her face look like she had a makeup artist prepare her for a *Vanity Fair* photo shoot. *Vanity Fair* is a glossy magazine that has full-page photos of movie stars and politicians. Mom bought a subscription to *Vanity Fair* over the telephone. She told me that 12 percent of her money went to help the Special Olympics. We go to cheer at the Special Olympics every year. Sarah's cousin Roger competed in the hurdles last year. He got second to last, but he jumped up and down and celebrated like he had gotten first.

Grandma closes her eyes and smiles until the sun is completely gone. She plays Puccini on the CD player, and Belly always climbs up onto the pillow next to her and watches the lights dance across the ceiling. It makes you forget that Grandma is lying in a hospital bed and has cold feet.

Grandma always sings a song about froggies going to school to Belly. Belly stares at her mouth and touches Grandma's lip with her finger while she sings.

"'Twenty froggies went to school. . . .'"

When I was Belly's age, Grandma used to babysit me. She'd put an afghan around me that smelled like she did, like Estee Lauder perfume and freshly cut grass. She'd rock me back and forth in her chair and sing my favorite song, "Little Joe the Wrangler." It's about a little cowboy who ends up getting crushed by his horse.

I'm not sure why I liked it so much, but when she finished singing it, I'd say, "Sing it again, Grandma."

She usually had to sing it five or six times before I would fall asleep. I heard her singing it to Belly the other day.

Grandma doesn't let Dad close the curtains until it is pitch-black outside.

"I don't want to miss anything," she says to Dad.

Grandma says that summer is her favorite time of year. She used to have a flower garden that was full of peonies, roses, and lavender. It was in her garden where Grandma taught me how to use the bathroom outside. I was three years old, and she said that anytime I was in her garden and had to go, I should just stop where I was and pee. I peed on her peonies. I peed on her tulips. I peed in her birdbath. Then Grandma told me that she preferred it if I just peed in the dirt. I liked to go to the bathroom outside better than I did inside. Whenever I was watching television with India and had to use the restroom, I'd run outside and go off the back porch, instead of running down the hall to the toilet. This ended when Mom took me to the flower shop and I got confused. I thought I was outside and ended up peeing in a vase of calla lilies.

Mom has never been back to that store.

Grandma misses her garden. She talks about it all the time. Uncle Max brought over all her old gardening books and photographs of her gardens from many years ago. In one of them she's standing next to a huge yellow rosebush. Mom is standing next to her. Mom looks like Belly, except her hair is brushed, there isn't dirt on her face, and she's wearing a shirt. Grandma looks like Mom does now, like she smells like tea and sandalwood.

One day the manny said he was going to take us to the nursery.

"We're a little old for the nursery, aren't we?"

I asked, trying to talk the way that Lulu does.

"Not a baby nursery, dodo," said Lulu. "A plant nursery."

"I know. I was just joking," I said.

But I wasn't.

The manny had come up with a brilliant plan, or at least that's what Dad said. We were going to transform the backyard into a beautiful flower garden for Grandma to look out of her window at. Even Lulu liked the idea, but she said that she had thought of it first, she just hadn't said it out loud.

Right now the backyard has our old rusted swing set and a big tractor-tire sandbox in it. We can't play in the sandbox because all the neighborhood cats use it as a communal litter box. We discovered this when Belly came into the house one afternoon smelling like cat poop. Mom made her take a bath for an hour and then cleaned the tub with Clorox when she was done.

At the nursery the manny let us pick out flats of flowers and a huge pot to take care of as our very own. Lulu picked something called chocolate cosmos because they smelled like and were the same color as chocolate. India picked daisies. She said that daisies were like "sunshine growing out of the dirt." Belly picked out yellow marigolds. I thought they were ugly, but they ended up living longer than any of the other flowers. I picked petunias. I hate the name, but I think that they are very pretty. They are Mom's favorite, too.

When we were finished picking out our own flowers, we walked through the aisles choosing flowers and plants for Grandma's garden. We picked lilies, a hydrangea, lavender, peonies, rosemary, mint, and a rosebush with yellow roses. The manny held up a bunch of hollyhock plants behind him like a peacock tail and cawed at the top of his lungs. The other shoppers moved to a different aisle and made sure their children were close to them.

The cashier rang it all up, and the manny used Uncle Max's credit card to pay for it. Uncle Max had sold a painting and wanted to be a part of our Grandma's Garden Surprise plan. He couldn't come with us, so he gave the manny his credit card. I watched how well the manny wrote Uncle Max's signature. He had beautiful handwriting. I bet the manny probably had to spend a lot of time after school writing sentences.

We left the nursery and went down to the riverbank, where we looked for rocks to line the flower beds with. Lulu decided that she was in charge of inspecting the rocks that we found. She said that we needed big, smooth rocks that were all around the same size. She said no to every rock that I picked out. The manny threw a rock into the river, which splashed Lulu. He pretended that it was an accident, but I think he did it on purpose, because after he did it, he said, "'I'm melting, I'm melting,'" like the Wicked Witch of the West from *The Wizard of Oz*.

Lulu quickly snapped back, "'I'll get you, my pretty.'"

Then she looked at me. "'And your little dog, too.'"

I laughed, but I don't think she really meant it as a joke, because she was grumbling after she said it. If she were a cartoon, there would have been a bubble coming out of her mouth with exclamation marks, question marks, and other bad-word marks. I wish she were a cartoon. I'd erase her so the manny would want to stay forever.

I stopped trying to find round, smooth rocks and started to look for rocks that were shaped like different states. I have a collection of twenty-four state-shaped rocks. I even have the Hawaiian Islands.

I found Oklahoma and shoved it into my pocket.

When we got home, we ate dinner and waited

for the sun to go down. We had to wait until Grandma would let Dad close the curtains before we could start planting the surprise garden. We didn't want her to see us. This meant we had to use flashlights and whisper like we were spies.

Finally the sun was going down, and Grandma and Belly were drifting to sleep in the big, shiny hospital bed. The manny grabbed flashlights, and we began the transformation. First we planted our own private flowerpots and placed them along the porch right outside of Grandma's window. We tiptoed. Then we dug all the sand out of the tractor tire and replaced it with soil that we had bought in bags. The manny tripped over the tire and fell right on his back with a thud. I tried to cover my laughter so that I wouldn't wake Grandma up, but it made me have to go to the bathroom.

My first pee in Grandma's new garden.

While I tried to control my laughter, we planted the hydrangea bush in the middle of the tire. Lulu and the manny began to arrange different flower beds, using the river rocks as the edges. They left enough room so that Grandma's wheelchair could roll through the middle. Lulu kept telling the manny what to do, like she was in charge. The manny didn't look like it bothered him. His face stayed calm. He says that he's really good at looking "collected," and that's why he has a good chance of winning the National Poker Finals next year in Las Vegas.

We planted the rosemary, the mint, and the rest of the flowers in the river-rock-lined beds.

Uncle Max brought over an old birdbath that he had found at a flea market. Uncle Max calls the stuff he buys at flea markets "treasures." Grandma calls the stuff "trash." The birdbath was painted white and had a fancy base on it. It reminded me of something that might have been in the Snow Queen's garden from the Chronicles of Narnia. Last Christmas, India was in a play called *The Lion, the Witch, and the Wardrobe* that was based on the Chronicles of Narnia. She played a little girl who was turned into a stone statue. Every night after dinner she practiced standing completely still, even her face. She looked like the plastic mannequins from the front window of Saks Fifth Avenue. I tried to make her laugh by mooning her, but Mom told me to stop because I was teaching Belly inappropriate things. I got into *big* trouble during India's performance because Belly turned around on her chair, pulled up her green velvet dress, and pulled down her white tights to moon India, who was up on the stage pretending to be a statue.

I said to Mom, "India was really good. She never even *cracked* a smile."

Mom didn't think my joke was funny. I had to unload the dishwasher for a whole month.

Once the birdbath was filled with water, the manny cooed like a dove and plunged his face into the water. Uncle Max laughed at the manny and rubbed the back of his hair the same way he rubs mine when I do something funny.

I was glad that Lulu didn't see him do it, because I knew she'd write it in "The Manny Files."

The manny and Uncle Max said that they would be back in the morning before Grandma woke up.

They left.

I hung my clothes for the next day on my clothes valet and wrote in my journal.

June 27

The manny was funny today at the nursery. He dragged his knuckles along the ground and went, "Oo, oo, ahh, ahhh, ahhh," like an orangutan when he saw a banana plant. Lulu pretended to be with another family. A boy that she knew from school was in there with his mother. When they said hello to each other, the manny started whistling "Someday My Prince Will Come." Lulu spent the rest of the time at the nursery behind a big lilac bush writing in "The Manny Files."

We stopped at the Tastee-Freez to get ice cream, but I didn't get out of the car. Craig was there. I saw him say hi to the manny, but I ducked down when he looked over at the Eurovan. I don't think that he saw me.

Grandma will be so surprised tomorrow when she sees the garden that we planted for her. I bet it makes her feet warm.

Born on this day: Helen Keller, Ross Perot, Captain Kangaroo

I pressed a petunia from my flowerpot in between the pages of my journal and fell asleep.

16 Cucumber Sandwich

The next morning I woke up to the smell of bacon coming from the kitchen. I disrobed my clothes valet, hung my pajamas where my clothes had been, put on my watch, and ran down the stairs into the kitchen.

Mom and Dad were sitting at the kitchen table in their robes having coffee. India sat next to them in her silk kimono from Uncle Max. She had her legs crossed like Mom's. She was sipping apple cider, but I could tell that she was pretending that it was coffee. The *New York Times* was spread out all over the table. Mom had the Week in Review. Dad had the Sunday Style section. India had the special *Fashion of the Times* magazine insert. She flipped through the pages of unsmiling models with their jeans slung low around their waists.

"I hope washing your hair comes back into fashion again soon," she said, shaking her head and sipping her apple "coffee."

Uncle Max was standing at the stove frying bacon and sausage in a pan. Lulu was next to him scrambling eggs.

She whined, "That's so gross. Look at all that grease. I would never eat bacon. Pigs are disgusting."

She grabbed a sausage and shoved it into her mouth.

Uncle Max shriveled up his nose and said, "Oink! Oink! I guess you think sausage is a vegetable."

Lulu, remembering what she had just said about pigs, pretended to be disgusted. She spit the chewed sausage into the sink and ran the disposal. She poured an entire glass of milk down her throat, the same way I do when I have to take cough medicine. It never even touches my tongue.

While Uncle Max made bacon and sausage, and Lulu scrambled eggs, the manny made toast. He asked me to go and get the breakfast-in-bed tray that I had gotten Mom for Mother's Day. Mom kept it in the hall closet, where she keeps her grandmother's china and where Dad used to hide his cigarettes. He quit smoking when Belly was born.

I got the breakfast-in-bed tray from the hall closet and took it in to the manny. We put eggs and bacon on a big plate. We put toast on a small plate. And we put Grandma's pills on a little tiny plate from Belly's tea party set. Uncle Max poured coffee into Grandma's Charlie Brown mug that says GOOD GRIEF. It was a gift from her friend June, who'd gotten it for her after the water bed hip-injury fiasco.

I learned the word *fiasco* from Ms. Grant during our school's Halloween parade through town. I was dressed up as airport security. I even had a pretend metal-detecting wand that made *beep, beep* noises. We lined up, like we always do, from shortest to tallest. Ms. Grant was dressed up as Little Bo Peep and had on a huge, frilly skirt that was held out with a hoop at the bottom. She led our class through the streets, which were lined with our parents. I, of course, was first in line behind her. Two blocks into the parade, while I was waving at Mom, I accidentally stepped on the back of Ms. Grant's long, frilly hoopskirt. She fell down, and before I could stop myself, I fell on top of her. The kids behind me were all waving at their parents, so nobody was paying attention. One after another my classmates piled on top of Ms. Grant. It was a dog pile of witches, ghosts, and Raggedy Anns. We climbed, one by one, off of Ms. Grant, who couldn't get up on her own because of the big hoopskirt. She just rolled around with her frilly, bloomer-covered legs kicking in the air until Mr. Allen grabbed her underneath her arms and pushed her back onto her feet.

"What a fiasco," she had said to Mr. Allen.

Lulu carried the breakfast-in-bed tray in to Grandma, who was looking at a garden book with Belly. Belly was petting the side of Grandma's cheek while Grandma flipped through the pages.

"Oh, my word," said Grandma when she saw Lulu carrying the tray. "What a nice treat." Belly grabbed a piece of bacon and shoved it into her mouth.

"Just wait," I said, running to pull open the curtains.

India went to the other side, and we opened them together.

"Taa-daa," I said.

Grandma's eyes lit up when she saw the purples, pinks, and yellows.

"How beautiful," she said, with her hands clasped together by her chin. Her eyes looked like Mom's do when she chops onions.

Grandma ate breakfast and spent the rest of the morning looking at her new garden.

At lunchtime Grandma felt good enough to get into her wheelchair. Dad and Uncle Max rolled Grandma out onto the back porch, while the manny and I pretended to be traffic cops. We waved Grandma in for a landing, until finally the manny blew on a shiny whistle and motioned her to stop.

I don't know where he got the whistle, but I want one.

Dad and Uncle Max lifted Grandma and her wheelchair down the three steps so that she was in the yard. Lulu, India, and I took turns wheeling Grandma through the garden and telling her how we had gone to the nursery and planted everything in the dark while she was asleep. I even told her about the manny splashing Lulu with water at the river.

"Did she deserve it?" Grandma asked.

I looked over to see if Lulu was listening. She wasn't. I turned to Grandma and nodded my head yes.

Grandma loved the garden. I could tell by the way she kept gasping and covering her hand with her mouth.

We ate a garden lunch.

The manny said it was very civilized to eat crustless tomato and cucumber sandwiches in the garden. We washed them down with lemonade.

While we were having shortbread cookies, I stood next to Grandma's wheelchair and she put her arm around me. Uncle Max took a picture of us with his Polaroid camera. We were next to the rosebush, just like in the picture of her and Mom when Mom was little.

"Say 'cucumber sandwich,'" said Uncle Max.

"Cucumber sandwich," we said, smiling really big. Grandma squeezed the back of my neck, and I got goose bumps.

I put the picture of Grandma and me in the Saks Fifth Avenue box in my top drawer.

June 28

Grandma was so excited about the garden. She said that if I watered them every day and if there was plenty of sun, the peony bushes would grow to be very tall. I decided to drink lots of water this summer and spend time in the sun to see if I would grow as tall as the peony bushes. I stood next to the doorframe, and the manny measured my height with a little hatch mark. I put June 28 next to it so that I can see how fast I'm growing. Maybe I won't have to be first in line next year.

Born on this day: John Elway, Henry VIII, Gilda Radner (the girl from *Saturday Night Live* who says, "That's so funny I forgot to laugh")

17 I Bet They Put June's Bra in the Freezer

We still planned a summer vacation, even though Grandma was living in our living room. June and the other canasta ladies said they would take turns staying over with her while we were gone. Virginia said she'd make a special trip to the liquor store. Mom didn't like the sound of that. She left a list of rules for Grandma, the same way she does for us when we stay at home alone while she and Belly run to the grocery store.

1. Don't let strangers into the house.
2. Don't tell strangers that you are home alone over the telephone.
3. Be responsible.
4. NO WILD PARTIES.

Mom never puts the last rule on our list of rules, but she put it in all capitals on Grandma's. Grandma told her not to worry, that she was looking forward to a quiet week of reading and resting. Then she winked at me when Mom wasn't looking.

This year we went fly-fishing and camping on a river in the mountains. Dad says summer vacations are for introducing us to what the world has to offer. Last year we went to Disneyland and I threw up cotton candy on the teacups. He said that cotton candy and throwing up were two of the things the world had to offer. The year before that we went to Venice, Italy. Belly was a little baby, and Mom bought her a black-and-white-striped gondolier outfit. When we took a gondola ride through the canals, people pointed at Belly from the arched bridges above. They called her adorable and precious. I thought she looked like a tiny prisoner, except she needed ankle shackles. We wouldn't have as many broken things in our house if Belly wore ankle shackles.

Uncle Max and the manny were invited to come along on the fly-fishing trip. I couldn't wait. The manny *always* seems like he's on vacation. I couldn't imagine what he'd be like when he really was. A week before the trip I packed everything I would need into my backpack. Sunglasses. Shorts. My journal. I put the back-pack in the corner of my room with a note on it to myself. It said, "Don't forget to pack your toothbrush." The manny added "And razor and shaving cream" to my note.

Mom and Dad spent the evenings of the week before our trip packing sunscreen, flashlights, and life jackets and getting together medical kits in case of an emergency. Dad knew what he was doing. When he was in college, he spent his summers as a fly-fishing guide. He guided tourists in boats down rivers. Most of the tourists that he guided had never been fishing before. He said they were wild with their fishing rods, and he had to lie completely down in the boat sometimes so that they wouldn't hit him with the hook. One time someone fell out of the boat as they floated through rapids. I must have looked worried, because Dad said, "Don't worry. We're only floating on calm water. Nobody will fall out of the boat unless they are pushed."

"Good idea, Dad," I said as Lulu walked through the room, modeling her new rain gear.

He didn't hear me.

The day we left for the mountains, Wanda, Thelma, Virginia, and June came over to see us off. They had luggage with them. Thelma told Mom that they all had decided to stay over with Grandma until we returned. She told Mom that it would be like a slumber party. Mom looked worried but shrugged her shoulders and continued putting our backpacks, tents, and life jackets into the back of the Eurovan.

The manny whispered in my ear, "I bet they put June's bra in the freezer while she's sleeping."

I whispered back, "I don't think it will fit."

The manny snort-laughed.

When Dad and Uncle Max were finished securing the boat to the top of the Eurovan, the manny yelled, "All aboard." We ran into the house to give Grandma and the canasta ladies hugs. Grandma kissed me on the forehead. It left a wet mark, but I didn't wipe it off. When we ran back outside, Mom and Dad were already in the front seats of the Eurovan. Lulu and India got in the back, and Belly got into her car seat. I rode with Uncle Max and the manny in Uncle Max's Honda Accord. It's much cleaner than our Eurovan, which has lollipop sticks from the bank stuck to the ceiling. It was a day's drive to the mountains, five days of camping, and a day's drive back home.

Uncle Max drove all morning, and Mom drove the Eurovan. Uncle Max and the manny sang along to the radio. They competed to see who knew the words to the most songs. I kept score in the backseat. The manny won. He even knew the words to some country songs. Uncle Max said that he didn't want to win if it meant that he had to listen to country music. The rest of the day the manny tuned the radio to a country station and sang with every song, while Uncle Max groaned.

The manny wailed, "'I've got friends in low places, where the whisky drowns and the beer chases my blues away.'"

Uncle Max said, "If you don't stop singing, I'm going to drive this car into oncoming traffic."

The manny said that if he was going to record a country album, he needed the support of his friends. Then he laughed and started singing louder.

When it was time for lunch, Mom pulled into a little burger place where you ordered from a window and then ate outside at picnic tables. Uncle Max pulled the Honda Accord in right next to the Eurovan. Belly did a blowfish against the window at us. Uncle Max did one back. It left lip marks on the window, but he wiped them off with his shirt. Belly didn't wipe her lip marks off the Eurovan window. They will probably be there until she's twelve.

We ordered our burgers and sat at the picnic table and ate them. It was so warm that Belly took her shirt off. She looked like a street urchin because she had eaten her cheeseburger straight through the middle, and it left a ketchup stain from the corners of her mouth all the way up to her ears. We watched *Oliver* last year in music class. Oliver was a street urchin, but even he somehow managed to stay cleaner than Belly does.

Lulu finished her lunch first and opened her backpack to find her walkman to listen to. When she unzipped her backpack, I noticed the corner of "The Manny Files" sticking out of the top. I couldn't believe that she had brought it along on a camping trip. I guess some things you just don't take a vacation from.

When we had all finished lunch, Mom stood up and stretched her arms over her head. Her shirt came up, and I could see her belly button and her scar from where they had to take Belly out of her. It's next to her belly button, and she calls it her Belly zipper. We got back into the cars, only this time Dad drove the Eurovan and the manny drove Uncle Max's Honda Accord.

Belly gave us one more cross-eyed blowfish against her window, and then the Eurovan pulled out and led us down the highway. The manny followed Dad, while Uncle Max and I played a drawing game. One of us would draw a squiggle on a notepad, and then the other had to make a picture out of it. I turned most of Uncle Max's squiggles into boats, and he turned most of my squiggles into faces. After a while Uncle Max fell asleep. The manny put in an Andrea Bocelli CD and kept driving. He called it the "soundtrack for the landscape."

I fell asleep too.

When the manny woke us up, we were parked next to the Eurovan again. This time Belly was pressing her bare bum against the window at us. Mom got mad and made her quit. I saw Lulu saying something to Mom. I bet she was telling her that the manny let Belly moon other cars through the window of the Eurovan. He doesn't.

We were parked in a pullout where our camping trip would end. Uncle Max, the manny, and I got out of the Honda and into the Eurovan. We left Uncle Max's car there so we would have a car at the end of the trip. I dashed over to Mom and whispered that the manny didn't teach Belly how to moon people.

"What are you talking about?" said Mom.

"Never mind," I said. Lulu must have been talking about something else.

We had ten miles until we reached the spot

that Dad planned on launching our boat. We weren't floating very far each day because we wanted to fish and swim. Mom needed to relax. She had just finished hosting a show at the museum where she had to ask people to donate money so they could get new carpets. I had given her six dollars.

In the Eurovan we were one seat belt short, so the manny and I double-buckled. Mom said that normally this wouldn't be okay, but Dad was going to drive very carefully and it was only ten miles. She worries about teaching us bad things. Dad didn't drive as carefully as Mom wanted him to. She kept telling him to slow down.

When we got there safely, Mom told us again that double-buckling wasn't something we should do. It was three o'clock, and the river was a short walk from where we parked the Eurovan. Dad and Uncle Max got the boat off the top of the van. Mom and the manny began unloading the ice chests and backpacks and carrying them down to the river. I helped them. India was in charge of Belly. Lulu didn't help. She sat on the rocks by the river and wrote in "The Manny Files." The manny had started throwing rocks into the river and saying to Belly, "Did you see that fish?" She stared at the river but never saw a fish. I guess Lulu thought it was mean and needed to be documented.

When the boat was loaded and the Eurovan was locked up, we put our life jackets on and chose our spots in the boat. I sat up front next to India and Belly. Dad was right in the middle where the big oars were so he could guide us to our first camping spot. Uncle Max and the manny shoved us away from shore and then jumped into the boat.

Lulu squealed, "Wait! My notebook!" and pointed at "The Manny Files," which was lying on the rocks right where she had been writing in it.

The manny quickly jumped out of the boat and into the knee-deep water. He ran on shore, grabbed the notebook, and bolted back for the boat. Dad tried to keep the boat close to shore, but it was still waist deep by the time the manny got close enough to hand Lulu her manny slam book. She didn't even thank him until Mom pointed out that she hadn't.

"Thanks," she said without even looking at the manny, who was now sitting in the boat in his wet shorts. Uncle Max grabbed a towel and dried off the manny's legs.

Even though she had said thanks, I knew she didn't mean it. She must really hate the manny (or in Mom's words, the manny must really bug her). I don't know why she doesn't like him. He must like her, or he wouldn't have saved "The Manny Files."

We didn't fish on the first day. Dad said that we were not going very far and we should just enjoy being outside. The water was cold. India and I dragged our hands in it as the boat slowly wound through the canyon. The river was walled in on both sides with tree-covered mountains. The trees were great big Douglas firs and looked like they were a hundred years old. Above the trees was blue sky with fluffy white clouds that looked like floating marshmallows. Belly lay on her back and looked up at them, before the gentle rocking of the boat put her to sleep. Everyone was quiet. Instead of talking, we just looked around. There were no power lines, no buildings, and no other people. I felt like I do right before I fall asleep, when I know I'm drifting, but I also know I'm still awake. I swayed back and forth like drunk people do in the movies. I snapped out of it when I saw a deer at the edge of the river getting a drink. Dad stopped rowing, and we floated by it silently. It watched us just as much as we were watching it.

After a couple of hours we reached our first campsite. There was a designated spot for tents and a big metal box to put our food in so the bears wouldn't get it.

"Are there bears out here?" I asked India.

India answered, "I think so, but they won't bother us if we keep our food put away."

The manny said, "If we see one, I'll kick Uncle Max in the shin, and then we can all make a run for it. You don't have to be a fast runner, you just have to be faster than your friends."

Mom laughed, but Lulu said, "Let's kick you in the shin."

I think I was the only one who heard her.

We set up our tents while Mom and Lulu prepared dinner. Mom, Dad, Belly, and I were in one tent. India and Lulu were in another tent. And Uncle Max and the manny were in a tent. Their tent was the smallest. It was really a one-person tent, but they said they could manage.

We had turkey sandwiches and Oreo cookies for dinner. We basically had sandwiches for lunch and dinner every day. Dad built a fire, and we sat around it and told stories and ate cookies until it was dark. Belly and Mom were already asleep in the tent when Dad and I came in. I heard Uncle Max make a bear-growling sound and India and Lulu scream and then laugh. I popped my head out of the zipper opening in the tent to see, but all I saw were Uncle Max and the manny sitting by the fire, which now was just red-hot embers. I climbed back into the tent and into my sleeping bag. I turned on my flashlight and started to write in my journal.

July 6

We're camping beside a river. The manny came with us, just like he is part of the family. I can hear Uncle Max talking to him right now. I can't hear what they're saying because the sound of the river drowns it out.

Lulu almost lost "The Manny Files" today. She left it on the side of the river when we got into our boat. I saw it before we left, but I didn't say anything. I was hoping it would be left behind and gone forever. The manny saved it. I guess he doesn't understand the seriousness of Lulu and how she got Amy fired. Maybe Lulu will leave it somewhere again or I'll have a chance to tie a rock to it and sink it to the bottom of the river when nobody is looking.

Tomorrow Uncle Max is going to swim in the river with me. He promised.

Born on this day: Frida Kahlo, Janet Leigh, Sylvester Stallone

I put my journal back in my backpack, turned off the flashlight, and snuggled into my sleeping bag. I couldn't hear Uncle Max and the manny anymore. Dad put his arm around me and I fell asleep.

Don't Be Such a Green Butt Skunk

When I woke up the next day, I was the only one in the tent. I put on my fleece pants, socks, and Teva sandals and crawled out. Everybody else was already awake, and the other tents were already broken down. The adults were drinking coffee. Dad called it camp coffee. It was dark black, so it looked like they were drinking tar. Lulu, India, and Belly were eating bacon and toast. I guess Lulu had forgotten that she didn't like bacon. The manny was frying the bacon over the fire. Dad started to break down our tent.

After breakfast it was warm enough to wear our swimsuits. We put them on with our life jackets while Mom and Dad packed the boat. We were fishing today, and Dad had the fishing rods and flies unpacked and on the floor of the boat. This time before the manny shoved us away from the bank, he went through a checklist to make sure that we had everything. Backpacks . . .

check. Sunscreen . . . check. Good attitudes . . . check.

We shoved away from the bank and started to float down the river. India lathered sunscreen on her shoulders and then gave me the extra that was left on her hands. The manny wore a bandanna on his head like a motorcycle rider. He said if he didn't, his head would get sunburned and he'd look like a thermometer.

"You kind of already do," I said.

He laughed a great big sarcastic laugh that was funnier than my joke.

Once we were out in the river and on our way, Dad tied a fly to his fly rod. Dad's flies have funny names. His favorite is called a Green Butt Skunk. We started using it in conversation.

"Oh, Uncle Max, don't be such a Green Butt Skunk," I said when he splashed me with water.

"I'm as tired as a Green Butt Skunk," said India before she curled up on the floor of the boat to take a nap.

"I love you, my Green Butt Skunk," Mom said to Belly, who rubbed her face up against Mom's arm like a kitten.

After only a few minutes of floating Dad dropped the anchor into the water and the boat stopped. He stood up and started casting his line out into a spot where the water was dark and looked deep. I watched the fly touch the surface of the water twice, and then it sat there and floated down the river. After three casts Dad hooked a fish. It didn't take him very long to reel it in because it was really little. He called it a par. Belly squealed and buried her head in Mom's armpit when Dad held it up for her to see. India thought it was cute. She held it for a second under the water and then let go and watched it swim away. We don't keep the fish we catch. We let them go so they can get bigger and maybe we'll catch them again in a few years. It's called catch and release.

Dad looks like he's dancing when he casts his fishing rod. I look more like I'm having seizures. Dad handed me the rod, and I pretended to know what I was doing. I swung the silver line back behind my head and then swung it forward again. The entire boat screamed, and Mom covered Belly with her body. Lulu sank way down in the boat and put a life jacket over her head to protect herself from my flying hooks. The hook slammed into the back of my life jacket, knocking me forward a little bit. It felt like somebody had swatted me on the back. It didn't hurt, but it did scare me. I held back tears by clearing my throat.

"Nice cast," said Lulu, poking her head out from underneath the life jacket and laughing like it was the most ridiculous thing she'd ever seen. Mom squeezed Lulu's leg to make her stop, but Lulu pulled away and looked at Mom as though she didn't understand what the big deal was. I could feel my ears heating up, and my face started itching like it was burning red.

Dad said that bad casts happen to everyone and it just takes a lot of practice. I decided I didn't want to practice or fish anymore.

I handed the rod to India, who said, "No, thank you. I think it hurts the fish, and I don't want to be any part of it." Then she squashed a mosquito that had landed on her arm.

"Got it!" she yelled.

Lulu grabbed the rod and said, "I'll show you how to do it," in her snottiest Green Butt Skunk voice. I sat down and looked across the water, away from everybody, so they wouldn't see my teary eyes.

Lulu looked like Dad with the fishing rod, throwing it back and forth like a lariat. Mom didn't even cover Belly's head as a precaution. Instead she reached into her bag and grabbed the sunscreen for us to reapply. Dad says Mom is obsessive about sunscreen. Mom rubbed sunscreen all over Belly's legs until they were white, then she squeezed a little bit into my hand.

As I rubbed the sunscreen into my forehead and across my nose, I heard Lulu announce excitedly that she could feel a fish on her line. She reeled it in, and then the fish swam away from the boat again, taking Lulu's line out farther. Dad calls this playing the fish. He says it tires them out, and then it's easier to reel them in and it doesn't tear up their mouth. Lulu played the fish for twenty-five minutes.

When she finally reeled the fifteen-pound salmon in to the net that Dad was holding, India and the manny were cheering. I pretended to have sunscreen in my eyes. I held my hands over my scrunched-up face and told Mom that I couldn't see. Lulu's good at everything. I couldn't believe that she had caught a fish. If I didn't look at the fish, then I could always accuse Lulu of fibbing about its size. I didn't uncover my eyes until I heard a big splash and knew that Lulu's fish had been returned to the wild. I never even saw it. Uncle Max and Belly were now cheering for Lulu, who had a big smile on her face (not a mean smile, but a happy one). It made me wish I had looked at her fish.

"Nice job, babe," Dad said to Lulu as he pulled the anchor out of the water and into the boat. "That's enough fishing for now. Let's float for a little while."

The manny stretched his legs out and put his arms behind his head. So did I. He winked at me. I could tell even though he had silver wraparound sunglasses on and a red bandanna on his head. He looked like he belonged on a Harley-Davidson. Sarah's uncle has a Harley-Davidson, and he gave us rides around the yard one time. Sarah's mom screamed during her ride like she was on a roller coaster.

We floated for an hour before we came to a big rock in the middle of the river. It was high enough to climb, and the water below it was deep enough to jump into. Dad anchored the boat right next to the rock, and we took turns jumping. Mom and Belly stayed in the boat. Belly thought the water was too cold. India and Lulu jumped in first and came up screeching and dog-paddling toward the boat. Dad and I jumped at the same time. Uncle Max did a cannonball and splashed Belly and Mom, who yelled at him in a pretend-mad voice.

The manny said, "Watch this. This is the dive that won me the gold medal in the 1984 Olympics." He did a flip. It *was* good, but it wasn't Olympic-gold material. Or at least that's what India told him.

When the manny pulled himself into the

boat, his swimsuit came down a little in the back, and you could see his tan line and the very top of his crack. Mom calls it butt cleavage when it happens to Belly.

Uncle Max started howling like a wolf.

"What are you doing?" asked India, shaking her head like he was crazy.

"Howling at the *moon*," said Uncle Max.

The manny climbed into the boat and tugged his swimsuit up. He tied the drawstring and stuck his tongue out at Uncle Max.

We hadn't floated for very much longer when we stopped for lunch. While we were eating peanut butter and jelly sandwiches, I saw another deer in the woods behind our lunch spot. I didn't tell anyone. It was my secret deer. It stared at me like it wanted to come home with me, but it ran off when Belly screamed. An ant was crawling close to her. Belly's scared of ants, roly-polies, and Santa Claus. Last Christmas, Mom took Belly to meet Santa Claus and get her picture taken with him for our Christmas cards. When Mom lifted Belly onto Santa's lap, Belly started kicking and flailing wildly and screaming, "I hate Santa! I hate Santa!" Mom said the other mothers acted shocked and looked at her like she was a disgrace to the evolutionary chain.

Belly accidentally flung her elbow into Santa's nose, which started to bleed. Some of the other kids started to cry when they saw Santa bleeding all over his white fluffy beard. The elves tried to comfort the kids, but they smelled like cigarette smoke, and nobody wanted to talk to them. Mom showed us the pictures that night at dinner. Santa had a bloody Kleenex shoved in his nose. Belly was on his lap in midscream, with tears streaming down her face and a wet spot on the front of her pants. Mom sent the picture only to Uncle Max and Grandma. Grandma has it framed on her desk.

After lunch we got in the boat and launched away from the bank. Lulu told the manny that she thought his hairy chest was gross. She didn't say anything to Dad or Uncle Max, who also have hairy chests. Lulu pulled out "The Manny Files" and started writing something about the manny's hairy chest.

The sun was so hot that Uncle Max, the manny, India, and I jumped off the side of the boat and floated next to it in our life jackets. The current made me feel like I was swimming super fast. We swam in circles around the boat. I kicked my feet harder when I was by Lulu so it looked like I was accidentally splashing her. It got some of her pages that she was working on wet. I hoped it ruined them. Mom knew it wasn't an accident and told me to knock it off or I couldn't swim anymore. I stopped because I wanted to keep swimming. We climbed back into the boat and jumped off as many times as we wanted to. It was our own floating dock. It was so much fun that we didn't fish anymore that day. I was glad. I didn't want to fish ever again.

We reached our second campsite by four o'clock. This campsite had a sandy beach that Dad and Belly napped on. Mom, Lulu, India, Uncle Max, the manny, and I went for a little hike. We saw bear scat! Scat is what Uncle Max calls poop. Lulu stepped in the scat, but I didn't tell her. I let it hang on the back of her heel for a few minutes before it fell off.

Lulu walked in the front of the line, and Uncle Max and I were at the very back. I quietly asked Uncle Max if he knew why Lulu disliked the manny so much. I was hoping Uncle Max would tell me that Lulu was just mean and hateful, or that Lulu was mentally unstable and was on medication, but instead he gave me a real answer.

He said, "Lulu is at an age where she's

between being a little girl and a woman. People Lulu's age are just figuring out who they are and who they want to be. Lulu's body is changing, and it's probably weird to have a man hanging around all of the time, especially a man like the manny, who does things that bring attention. Lulu just wants to fit in and not stick out in the crowd, and I think the manny makes that hard for her."

"Oh," I said like I understood what Uncle Max was saying, but I don't think I did. I looked to the front of the line and saw Lulu and Mom walking next to each other. Lulu and Mom have the same walk. Lulu does look a lot more like Mom than she used to and less like India. Just then Lulu picked a wedgie. I've never seen Mom pick a wedgie.

When we returned from our hike, we woke up Dad and Belly. Belly had drool coming out of the corner of her mouth. I think she's going to snore when she gets older, like Lulu does.

Before bedtime we sat around the campfire. Uncle Max told a story about how when he and Mom were little, Grandma would let them sleep in a tent out in the backyard. One time they woke up in the morning to discover that the tent had been toilet-papered and a message had been written on the ground in shaving cream. It said YOU'RE SLEEPING ON MY GRAVE. When Uncle Max said this, Belly grabbed Mom's neck and squeezed so hard that Mom's head turned red and she had to free her neck from Belly's grip to breathe.

Uncle Max went on with the story, "We decided to sleep out in the tent the next night to see if we could catch the ghost. We had flashlights, a Polaroid camera, and a big sheet to capture the ghost with. It got later and later, and there was no ghost. At about two in the morning both your mom and I had grown tired of waiting and we fell asleep. Not very long after I woke up to the *pshhhh* sound of a shaving-cream can. I opened my eyes and could see the shadow of toilet paper blowing in the wind on the outside of our tent. I shook your mom awake and told her to get the camera. We were scared to death, but we wanted to find out whose grave we had been sleeping on. We peeked out of the opening of the tent and saw the back of somebody dressed in a dark robe, leaning down and writing a message on the ground. 'Now!' I yelled at the top of my lungs, and I charged out of the tent and tackled the ghost with the big white sheet. I tried to keep a hold of the ghost while it squirmed and wiggled wildly under the sheet. I could see the unfinished message written on the ground. It said SLEEP SOMEWHERE ELSE OR I WILL . . . When your mom was ready with the Polaroid, I uncovered the ghost's head and was blinded by the flash of the camera. Your mom screamed and I got scared. The ghost pulled away and ran around the house, taking the sheet with it. We hovered over the Polaroid picture to see if the ghost would show up on film. When it finally developed, there I was holding the sheet open to reveal your grandma clutching a can of shaving cream."

"Grandma was trying to scare you?" I looked at him with my eyes wide open in disbelief.

"Yes!" Mom said in a can-you-believe-it voice. Then Mom took over the story. "We ran into the house to catch her, but she was already under the covers, pretending that she had been asleep. She said that it must have been a bad dream and that we'd probably had too much soda to drink before bed. We knew it had been her, though. She was all sweaty, and there was a can of shaving cream on her nightstand."

"So the craziness is inherited?" said Lulu. "We don't stand a chance." She looked over at India, who shook her head in agreement.

"Time for all children with insane families to go to bed," said Mom.

"That's us," India said, grabbing my shoulder.

We wandered off to our tents, and I was too tired to write much in my journal. Instead I just opened it up and wrote:

July 7

Camping Trip

THE MOST FUN DAY OF MY LIFE, EXCEPT I HATE FLY-FISHING.

19 If Only I'd Worn My Toupee

The next morning when I crawled out of the tent, there was a message written in shaving cream on the ground. It said GOOD MORNING, KEATS! I'm not sure, but I think the manny wrote it, because he had a freshly shaved face. He denied it, but nobody would act as his alibi. An alibi is someone who can back up another person's story. I learned what an alibi was when Ms. Grant had lunchroom duty. I slipped on the water-covered tile floor, and my entire tray of turkey with mashed potatoes and gravy flew into the back of Ms. Grant's black slacks. She got mad and told me that I shouldn't be running in the lunchroom and I needed to stay after school. Sarah told her that I wasn't running, and Ms. Grant changed her mind about keeping me after school. She said, "It's good that Sarah's your alibi. She's very honest." Then Ms. Grant walked away with a big mashed-potato stain on her butt and gravy dripping down the back of her leg. Sarah covered her mouth and giggled, but I was too embarrassed to join her.

Even when Lulu claimed to have seen him do it, the manny denied writing the shaving-cream message. He said that he thought Belly did it.

"I did," said Belly, nodding her head yes, even though she can't write or even spell.

After breakfast we took our tents down and packed our things into the boat. Dad said that today was a big fishing day because we were going through deep pools that had lots of fish in them. I didn't care. I wasn't going to fish.

Mom was the first one to fish. She used a fly called the Hairy Mary. She said it was her lucky fly. Mom let Belly hold on to the rod with her while she cast. I guess it was lucky, because they caught a big fish that Dad guessed was twenty pounds. They called it Belly's fish, like she had actually caught it.

Belly even turned to me like I was her *younger* brother and said, "Are you going to fish? It's easy."

"Nope," I said without explaining, and I watched Belly's fish swim away.

Uncle Max took the fly rod and started casting. He used Mom's Hairy Mary fly because he liked the name. The fish he caught was a little smaller than Belly's fish, and he caught it in the gills, so it was bleeding all over the inside of the boat. Lulu held her nose and gagged and looked out the other side of the boat. Dad had to kill the fish by hitting it on the head with a stick. India looked like she was going to cry, but she agreed with Mom that the fish needed to be put out of its misery. Dad wrapped it in plastic and put it in the cooler. The manny took his hat off and held it over his heart. He said he was paying his respects. After we gave the fish a moment of silence, Uncle Max handed the fly rod to the manny, who switched from the Hairy Mary to the Stone Fly. Uncle Max was done fishing for the day. That's the rule of catch and release. If you kill a fish, you can't cast a rod for the rest of the day.

The manny had never been fly-fishing before, but you couldn't tell. He didn't cast as well as Dad, but nobody in the boat had to scream or duck out of the way of his hook. Except Lulu— she screamed every time he cast, but I think she was just trying to mess him up. She stopped screaming when the manny caught a fish.

The manny kept yelling "woohoo" as he reeled his first fish in to the boat. Uncle Max and I took turns high-fiving him, while India, Mom, and Belly held the fish in the water and petted its nose. Lulu wrote in "The Manny Files" and pretended like nothing was even happening. I pretended to fall into her and tried to knock "The Manny Files" into the river, but Lulu clutched it to her chest and kicked me away with her foot. I almost fell in instead, but India grabbed me. The manny said that if I had fallen in, he would have used his expert fishing skills to catch me.

"We never would have seen Keats again," said Lulu. The manny laughed, even though Lulu meant it to be mean.

"This might be my new sport," said the manny as he cast his line out in the river. "You might read my name next to Ernest Hemingway's in the annals of great fishermen." Ernest Hemingway is Dad's favorite writer. He was a fisherman. Just as the manny had finished bragging, the hook smacked him in the back of the head with a louder crack than when it had hit my life jacket. The red bandanna flew off the manny's head, and I watched it float down the river. The manny gasped and yelped, "Sh— ouch!" I think he was going to say a bad word, but he stopped himself. The Stone Fly was lodged right in the back of the manny's head, and there was a little blood dripping down the back of his neck. Mom sat him down and went to work on dislodging the fly. She loves doing stuff like that. Her favorite things about being a mother are taking out splinters and peeling sunburned skin.

"If only I'd worn my toupee," said the manny.

"Be still," scolded Mom as she slipped the fly out of the manny's head and held it up like she'd won a competition. India started blotting the manny's head with a tissue that she had soaked in rubbing alcohol. Mom applied Neosporin and a Band-Aid over the cut. The Band-Aid was shaped like lips, so it looked like somebody with lipstick had kissed the back of the manny's head. Mom gave Belly the box of Band-Aids, and before we knew it, Belly's face was covered with lips.

I scooted over so the manny could join India and me in the people-who-don't-fish section of the boat, but he didn't sit down. Instead he picked up the fly rod and began fishing again! Within minutes he had a fish on his line. It was a big one too (bigger than Lulu's). He said that the big ones liked blood. Uncle Max took the manny's picture with it before he set it free.

The manny handed me the fly rod and said, "Do you want to get back up on your horse too?"

"Sure," I said, even though I wasn't sure at all.

I took the rod from the manny's hand and watched Lulu sink down into the boat and cover her head. India did too, but at least she waited until I wasn't looking. Belly stretched down on her stomach and covered the back of her neck and head with her arms like she was in a tornado drill.

They stayed in their positions while I cast wildly back and forth across the water. I hit the boat with the fly a few times, and Lulu screamed the same way she does when I chase her with a frog. Just when I was about to quit fishing, I felt a tug on the end of my line.

"I think you got one!" exclaimed Dad as he grabbed the net. Every time the fish tugged at the line, I felt like I was going to fall into the river. Uncle Max held on to me. I played the fish just like Lulu had done, letting it tire itself out before I reeled it in. Uncle Max grabbed the rod every once in a while to give my arms a rest. When the fish was close enough to the boat, Dad swooped it up with the net and unhooked it. Belly opened her eyes really wide when Dad held the fish up. It was almost the same size as her. Dad said it was at least thirty pounds. I was so excited that I couldn't speak. I just kept shaking my legs and petting the fish. It was shiny silver with rainbow colors. When I tried to speak, all that came out was nervous laughter.

Everybody cheered and congratulated me, even Lulu, who wanted to hold it to see what a thirty-pound fish felt like. Uncle Max took a picture of me with my fish, and I told him I wanted a copy for my journal. Lulu thought it was gross when I kissed the fish good-bye and watched it swim away. She told me she was never sharing a glass of water with me again.

The manny called me Papa the rest of the day. It was Ernest Hemingway's nickname.

July 8

I caught the biggest fish of the trip today. The manny argued with me that he actually had caught the biggest fish because he weighs 150 pounds and he caught himself. He hooked himself in the back of the head. Lulu told him that it would count only if we released him back into the river. The manny told her that she had a very quick sense of humor. She blushed. She likes compliments. Even from the manny.

We ate the fish that Uncle Max hooked in the gills for dinner tonight.

I can't wait to fish tomorrow.

Born on this day: John D. Rockefeller, Philip Johnson, Kevin Bacon

It was colder when I woke up the next morning, and I could hear rain pounding against the tent. We made breakfast (peanut-butter-and-jelly sandwiches) inside our tents and ate them while Mom and Dad decided if we were going to stay and wait until the rain stopped. Dad looked up toward the sky and said that he didn't think the rain was going to stop for a few days. I don't know how he knows things like this. He says it's because he was a Boy Scout. I was in Boy Scouts for a little while, and all we did was pick up trash along the side of the highway and talk about why drugs were a bad choice. We didn't learn the things that Dad learned, like how to build a boat out of sticks or which plants are poisonous to eat.

When the rain let up a little, Dad said that it was our chance to leave. We were going to float all the way to Uncle Max's Honda Accord and go home three days early. Dad said that everybody who wanted to fish had caught one, so we might as well head home. We packed up our bags. Lulu wrapped "The Manny Files" in the rain gear that she had brought for it, a big plastic bag.

Floating through the rain was fun, even though it was cold. Belly shivered, and Mom wrapped her arms around her to keep her warm. All you could see was Belly's face with her tongue hanging out, trying to catch raindrops in her mouth. India, Lulu, and I huddled together, and I watched the misty fog float through the trees. Lulu can be really nice when she wants to be.

The river looked mysterious, like in the books I've read about the Loch Ness monster. We floated for most of the day before we arrived at the car.

The manny and Dad had just pulled the boat out of the water when a crash of thunder shook the ground. Mom screamed and rushed Belly and India to the car. Lulu and I followed behind them.

Dad and Uncle Max quickly loaded the van with our tents, bags, and boat. Mom drove the Eurovan, and the manny drove Uncle Max's car. I rode with Mom and Dad this time because Mom said that Uncle Max and the manny needed some alone time.

How can they be alone if they're together? I thought, too exhausted to actually ask it outloud.

I didn't care. I slept the whole way home anyway.

It was midnight when we finally reached our street and I woke up. Mom told us that we needed to be extra quiet when we went inside because Grandma and her friends would be asleep and they weren't expecting us. We didn't want to scare them.

"What about unloading the boat?" I asked.

"We'll do all that tomorrow. Tonight just go in to bed," said Dad.

Uncle Max and the manny had already turned down another street. India said it was the street the manny lived on. India always knows everything. I think she might be a spy.

When we rolled into our driveway, there was a police car parked in it with its lights flashing and reflecting off the garage doors. All the neighbors were out on their porches and in their yards, curious about the commotion. Their faces were red from the police lights.

Mom worriedly rolled down her window and asked, "What's happened, Officer? Is everything okay?"

"Yes, ma'am," said the officer. "We were just

here on a disturbance-of-the-peace call, but everything is fine."

Mom let out a big breath.

The officer went on, "Apparently this is the third night in a row that loud music and laughing were coming from inside the house and disturbing the neighbors. When we got here, we expected to find a teenage party. We knocked on the door, and an older woman peered out through the curtain and yelled to her friends that it was 'the fuzz.' She let us in, and we found five older women playing cards and listening to the Beatles too loudly. They've promised to keep it down." The officer paused for a moment. "And to stop calling us the fuzz."

Mom thanked the officer, who got in his squad car and left. The disappointed neighbors went into their houses. They were probably hoping for a scandal, like if Lulu lost her mind and had to be taken away in a straitjacket.

I started singing, "'Bad boys, bad boys. Whatcha gonna do? Whatcha gonna do when they come for you?'"

Dad laughed.

Inside the house June, Thelma, and Wanda stumbled all over themselves apologizing to Mom. Virginia was on the back deck smoking a cigarette. She waved to us through the glass of the door.

The house was messier than usual, with seven empty wine bottles on the kitchen counter and empty pizza boxes on the kitchen table. There were cards strewn across Grandma, who was lying in her hospital bed.

Grandma didn't apologize. Instead she said, "What are you doing home so early, anyway? You look like a bunch of wet dogs."

"We'll tell you all about it in the morning," said Mom. "But now I have to get these kids to bed."

The canasta ladies promised to come clean our house bright and early the next morning, and they left. I hugged Grandma and went to my bedroom to change into dry, warm pajamas. I could still smell the red wine from Grandma's breath.

July 9

We're already back from summer vacation. It was the shortest one ever, but it felt the longest. It started raining, so we had to come home early. Right when I was starting to like fishing. I am glad that Uncle Max and the manny were there. I think Lulu is glad that Uncle Max was there too. Maybe once Lulu is comfortable with her new boobs, she'll want the manny around too.

The police were here when we got home because Grandma had a party that got out of control, even though it was just her canasta group. She didn't have to go to jail, but the policeman didn't like it when Grandma called him Fuzzy. I think she might have a police record now. I can't wait to tell the manny that Grandma is a felon.

Born on this day: David Hockney, Barbara Cartland, Tom Hanks

We spend most of the summer swimming at the pool at the golf and tennis club. Scotty's dad is the manager, so we always get free chips and drinks. Scotty takes swimming lessons every morning so that he won't have to wear his floaties anymore. I took swimming lessons last summer from a high school girl named Robin. She was really tan and her hair was the same color yellow as Dolly Parton's. During regular swimming hours she did fancy dives off the high dive. Every time she came up from underneath the water, she'd squeal, "My top came off. My top came off." The high school boys sat around her when she sunbathed.

One time Sarah and I were judging each other's dives off of the low board. I'm still too scared to go off of the high dive.

Sarah did a front flip.

I did a can opener.

Sarah did a perfect straddle jump.

I did a belly flop.

I thought it would be funny, and maybe even raise my score, if I came up out of the water squealing, "My top came off. My top came off." Sarah thought it was hilarious. She laughed so hard that she fell on the ground and rolled around. Robin, who was sunbathing on the cement by the high dive, didn't think it was as funny as Sarah did, especially when all the boys around her started to laugh. The next time she taught me swimming lessons, I had to tread water for five minutes.

It's hard to tread water when you're trying not to cry.

The manny takes us to the swimming pool when it's warm and sunny. We fill the Volkswagen Eurovan with blow-up toys, towels, and other kids from around the neighborhood. On the way to the swimming pool the manny sings, "'Summer lovin', had me a blast.'"

India always answers back, "'Summer lovin', happened so fast.'"

Lulu covers her ears and goes, "La, la, la," really loudly.

"Summer Nights" is a song from the movie *Grease*. We used to watch it all the time. India knew all the words to every song and would listen to the soundtrack in her room. She would shut her door, but we could still hear her wailing, "'Sandy, can't you see? I'm in misery.'"

We watched it so much that Mom sings one of the songs to Belly when she washes her hair in the kitchen sink. Belly cries when Mom washes her hair. I think that she's scared of the garbage disposal. I turned it on once when Mom was washing Belly's hair. Belly screeched and Mom got mad at me. I told her I had accidentally hit the switch with my elbow.

But I didn't.

Mom sings, "There are worse things I could do, than give Belly a shampoo."

Belly tries not to, but she always interrupts her sobs with giggles.

It sounds like this: "Whaaaaa-hee-hee-heee. Whaaaaa."

When we get to the swimming pool, the manny coats us all with sunscreen. He always says, "Protect your skin now, so you won't look like Uncle Max's leather briefcase when you grow up."

There's a lady at the pool who looks like

Uncle Max's leather briefcase. She lies by the pool every day. I saw some Dolce and Gabbana leather boots in Mom's *Vogue* magazine that would match her arms perfectly.

The manny wears blue zinc oxide on his nose and looks like an old-fashioned lifeguard in his red swimsuit. He calls them swim trunks. India wears a big sun hat tied to her head with a big navy blue ribbon. She sits on the side most of the time and reads a book. *Alice in Blunderland*, by Phyllis Reynolds Naylor. *Are You There God? It's Me, Margaret*, by Judy Blume, which the boys aren't allowed to check out of the school library for some reason. *D.V.*, Diana Vreeland's autobiography.

India swims whenever the manny swims. She wears a swim cap. She says that chlorine makes your hair "unmanageably dry and brittle." The manny doesn't use the stairs in the shallow end to get into the pool. He climbs the ladder to the high dive and then yells, "Geronimo," and does a huge cannonball that always gets the lifeguard wet.

Sometimes she blows her whistle at him.

I'm too scared to go off of the high dive. I wrote it down in my journal as one of my summer goals, right next to "Grow six inches."

The manny said that I should also put "Eat candy" and "Tease Lulu" on the list.

July 22

The manny took us to the swimming pool today. He did a cannonball off the high dive and splashed the lifeguard and had to sit out for five minutes. He told the lifeguard that it was an accident, but I was standing behind him and saw that he had his fingers crossed. After I saw the manny jump, I climbed up the ladder to go off the high dive. I stood there for so long that a line formed on the ladder. I got scared, and everybody had to climb back down the ladder to let me down. Craig was there and called me a weenie. I pretended not to hear him.

Checked my height chart by the door. I think I shrank. The manny said that sometimes staying in the water too long shrivels you up so much that you actually shrink.

Grandma has to take more pills. She looks like she's shrinking too. Her lips and hands are cold when she gives me kisses and hugs. Mom said that Grandma might have to go back to the hospital to get the blood circulating through her body better. I asked Mom if I might be sick because my feet got cold sometimes. She told me that Grandma always had cold feet and this was something different. I hope Grandma doesn't have to go. I like having her here.

Born on this day: Alex Trebek, Rose Kennedy, Oscar de la Renta

Grandma had to go back into the hospital because she has an "affection." Dad told me that the blood isn't pumping through her heart properly. The doctors at the hospital are going to do tests on her.

"Like the scoliosis and head lice tests at school?" I asked Lulu.

"No, dodo, like blood pressure and X-rays," Lulu snarled, barely looking up from "The Manny Files."

The manny asked the nurse at the front desk if he could get a quick collagen injection in his lips while he was there. Lulu didn't think that was funny. She added comments in her notebook and then scolded him, "You really should be thinking about Grandma at a time like this."

The manny turned to the nurse again and said, "Could Grandma get injections too?"

Lulu growled.

The manny and I stay in Grandma's room

when the nurses come to take her blood pressure and heartbeat. We make sure that they are doing it correctly. I learned what nurses are supposed do by watching Grandma's soap operas with her. On *General Hospital* all of the secrets come out when somebody is confined to a hospital bed. I keep waiting for a young woman to burst through Grandma's hospital door and announce that she is the baby that Grandma gave up for adoption thirty years before. I imagine that she introduces Grandma to her grandchildren, who have never met her and are much better looking than us.

The manny said that I would be an excellent soap opera writer when I grow up.

Grandma's hospital room is decorated with lots of Polaroid pictures that Uncle Max has taken. There's a picture of the manny and me jumping on the trampoline. We're laughing because I had just drooled. There's a picture of India looking like a Moroccan princess, watering Grandma's hydrangea bush. The big purplish blue flowers match India's turban. There's one of Lulu sitting at her lemonade stand. Lulu's lemonade stand didn't have much business. She charged people by the size of the house that they lived in. The bigger the house, the higher the price for a cup of lemonade. She had a big sign that said ICE-COLD LEMONADE: COST BASED ON A SLIDING SCALE. The manny bought ten cups. She didn't know what to charge him because she's never seen his house.

There's also a picture of Belly and Grandma taking a nap, with the afternoon sun shining into the living room onto their faces.

The manny said, "Since Grandma's in the hospital and can't be out in the world, we have to bring the world to her."

The world that we bring to Grandma is mostly cut flowers from her garden, soap opera magazines, and my Egyptian cotton sheets. Grandma needs them more than I do right now.

Sometimes I pretend to be Grandma's concierge. She'll ask where she can get a glass of water.

I say, "Oh, the tap water from the bathroom is fabulous."

When I bring Grandma her water, she slips tissues to me with a handshake, just like she did when she tipped the concierge at the Waldorf-Astoria in New York City.

The manny still dresses her up in different costumes to watch her soap operas. One day she was dressed up as an emergency room doctor. The manny had borrowed the uniform from the nurses' station. The nurses give the manny anything he wants. They like him because he calls them things like "beauty boat" and "heartbreaker" whenever they leave the room.

"Thanks for the extra pillow, dream girl," I heard him call after the big nurse that calls Grandma "honey."

When the doctor came into Grandma's room, she was lying in her bed wearing a pair of light blue hospital scrubs. She had a butter knife and fork in her hands and a surgeon's mask over her mouth. I had a shower cap on my head and looked like a nurse. The manny was sprawled out on the floor, pretending to be dead.

Grandma said, "I did all I could, but I am afraid that I just couldn't save him. All I could do was butter him with this cholesterol-free spread."

She waved the butter knife in the air.

The doctor laughed and said, "I see that it might be time to move you to the psychiatric ward. You could all share a room."

"It could be like *One Flew over the Cuckoo's Nest*," said the manny, "and Grandma could throw a drinking fountain through the window and we could escape."

I've never seen *One Flew over the Cuckoo's Nest,* but now I want to.

After two weeks in the hospital Grandma came back to live in our living room.

She didn't have surgery. Grandma told me she didn't want to be in the hospital anymore because the lighting was bad and made her wrinkles appear bigger than they actually were.

August 11

I'm so glad Grandma's living with us again. She can watch me water the garden from her bed in the living room. India says that Grandma is sicker than we thought. I'm going to rub her feet every day until she's better.

Craig rode by my house today on his bicycle. I was playing on the Slip 'N Slide with India. I waved to him, but he didn't wave back. He circled by a couple of times, but he never smiled or waved. I think he wanted to play on the Slip 'N Slide. The manny said it was probably because India was out in the yard in a swimming suit. She punched him in the arm when he said this. She also put a T-shirt on over her swimming suit.

Checked the height chart. I grew an eighth of

an inch. I marked it on the door. I thought I felt taller. Summer is almost over. Only another week left to jump off the high dive.

Born on this day: Hulk Hogan, Alex Haley, Jerry Falwell

This morning I gave Grandma a foot rub before the manny took us to the swimming pool. Her feet were colder than usual and she was asleep. I kissed her on the cheek and she smiled in her sleep. Then I ran upstairs to get my swimming suit. I wanted something very athletic looking because I was planning on jumping off of the high dive. I dug through my swimming-suit drawer and pulled out a red-white-and-blue one. I thought that if I wore it, I'd look like a firework exploding in the sky and plummeting into the pool.

On the way to the pool Lulu was complaining about the manny's Duran Duran CD that was playing. She says that they're completely out of style. She hates it when I point at her and sing, "'I'm on the hunt, I'm after you.'"

"Hungry Like the Wolf" is my favorite song of all time. My favorite song used to be "Hakuna Matata," from *The Lion King*, but that was when I was little.

India likes "The Reflex."

Whenever we're too loud in the van or Lulu is complaining, the manny yells, *"MUSHPOT!"* He usually does it when Lulu is in the middle of a sentence.

I bet that there's a whole page in "The Manny Files" about mushpot.

Whenever he yells this, the Eurovan goes completely silent. Mushpot means that nobody's allowed to make a noise. If somebody does make a noise, the rest of the van yells at the top of their lungs, "So-and-so's in the mushpot."

The longest we've ever lasted is three minutes and forty-eight seconds. Belly usually can't stand it and has to break the silence.

We were getting close to the swimming pool when Lulu said, "Please change the music before my friends he—"

"MUSHPOT!" yelled the manny.

India and I stopped talking about her sarong. Belly put both hands over her mouth and kicked her legs wildly with excitement. I could tell that she wanted to squeal. Lulu rolled her eyes and clenched her top lip with her teeth. She didn't like the game, but she didn't like to lose, either.

We sat in silence while "Wild Boys" blasted out of the van speakers.

I wanted to sing along, but didn't want to lose. I just pretended to drum along with the drum solo.

Belly looked out the window and forgot we were playing mushpot.

"Look, an airplane," she said, and pointed to the sky.

"Belly's in the mushpot," we yelled in unison.

"No, I'm not," she whined, then crossed her arms and stuck out her tongue.

She's a sore loser when we play mushpot.

We pulled up to the swimming pool, and everybody who was in line for the high dive looked over toward us.

"Her name is Rio and she dances on the sand . . . ," blasted from the open windows of the Eurovan.

We unloaded the bags of towels and sunscreen. Belly stopped just outside of the gate and started taking off all of her clothes. Kids pointed at her and laughed. Lulu pointed to the SWIMSUITS MUST BE WORN AT ALL TIMES sign.

Lulu hates rule breakers.

Sarah waved to me from the end of the high dive. She did a perfect pencil drop into the water. No splash. I ran over to meet her at the ladder.

"Isn't today the day you're supposed to jump off of the high dive?" asked Sarah.

I had told Sarah that if I didn't jump off of the high dive by August 16, I was never coming to the swimming pool again. I don't know why I chose August 16, it just popped into my head and out of my mouth.

We swam all afternoon. India sat on the side and flipped through the pages of the September issue of *Vogue* magazine. BIGGEST FALL ISSUE EVER, it said on its cover. India marked the pages that had ensembles that she liked.

Belly slept underneath a towel next to India.

Lulu sat on the other side of the pool by a boy named Fletcher and his friends. She had told India that Fletcher was the smartest, cutest boy in her grade. She doesn't know that India told the manny. Fletcher had freckles and a gap between his teeth when he smiled. He did really good dives off of the high dive.

I wish I had freckles.

The manny went to the concession stand to get India a Sprite. I went with him to help him carry. India sat with Belly to make sure that if she woke up, she kept her swimming suit on.

On his way to the concession stand the manny passed Lulu and Fletcher. Lulu was sprawled across the CONSTITUTION OF THE UNITED STATES beach towel that her friend Margo had brought her from Washington, D.C. She sat like somebody was taking her picture, with her arms behind her, her back arched, her knees together, and her legs crossed at the ankles. She had on a two-piece swimming suit. It was her first bikini. She had gotten her first bra a few months before. It looked like a tank top to me, except it was short and had a bow on the front. It didn't look like Mom's bras. Mom's bras are so big that they fit on my head like a hat.

Fletcher was lying on an old, bleached-out blue bath towel that had a hole in it. He was talking to the boy sitting on the other side of him and not to Lulu.

The manny looked at Fletcher, gave a thumbs-up sign, and said, "Wassup, dawg?"

"Nada, bro," said Fletcher.

The manny looked at Lulu.

Lulu didn't look back. I think she was hoping that the manny would go by without saying anything to her.

He looked at her and said, "Do you and your friends want anything from the concession stand?"

The color came back into Lulu's face and she said, "Sprites, please."

The manny and I came back with Sprites for Lulu and all her friends.

He said, "Catch you on the down low, homeslice," and he winked at Lulu.

As the manny walked away, Fletcher said, "That guy's cool. You're so lucky, Lulu. My aunt watches us, and she never takes her hair out of curlers, even when we go out to dinner. It's so embarrassing."

"Yeah, he's cool." Lulu squirmed uncomfortably and sipped her Sprite. I could tell she didn't mean it, but I could also tell that she was happy Fletcher was talking to her.

I said to Lulu, "You're so mean to him and he's so nice to you." She glared at me, so I ran to catch up with the manny. I dropped my Sprite and it spilled all over my feet and made them sticky. I jumped in the pool to wash them off.

I didn't want a Sprite anyway. My stomach felt just like it did the time we played baseball in PE and it was my turn to bat. I ended up hitting a foul ball that hit Mr. Rolls, our PE teacher, in the head. He had to go to the hospital to get stitches. Craig told me that I had probably killed him. We spent the rest of PE class in the library watching a film about caterpillars turning into butterflies.

I liked it, but I pretended to be bored.

Mr. Rolls had to get four stitches. My mom and dad sent him a gift certificate to a nice restaurant to say that they were sorry.

"Don't worry about jumping off the high dive," said Sarah. "It's not that bad."

"I know," I said. "I'm just waiting for the right moment. I don't want to wait in line."

Really I didn't want the line waiting behind me.

Just then the manny yelled, "We're leaving in five minutes."

"Guess you better do it," said Sarah with a worried look for me.

I climbed out of the pool, and my swimsuit fell down below my equator. That's what Uncle Max calls it when your crack shows. Lulu says that Uncle Max is childish sometimes. Mom always says he's childlike. I pulled up my suit and thought that this was not a good start. I walked over to the line for the high dive. I hate the line for the high dive. You have to stand on the ladder with your face right next to somebody else's bottom. I stood under Robin, my old swimming-lessons teacher. Water kept dripping from the bottom of her swimsuit onto my head.

I hoped it wasn't pee.

She turned around and said, "Are you just

climbing up for the view, or are you really going to jump this time?"

I said, "Your swimsuit top looks a little loose. You'd better tighten it."

She glared at me and climbed up the ladder.

It was finally her turn, and she gracefully dived from the board.

When she came up, she said, "Oh, my gosh!" and grabbed her top.

It was my turn. I climbed up onto the board and walked to the very end. Sarah was by the ladder. She looked like a toddler from that high. I looked down into the water and then back at the seven or eight people standing in line on the ladder.

They were already heckling me to go.

"Come on."

"Don't be a wimp."

Robin yelled, "Hey, Keats, do you want us to bring you your dinner up there?"

I looked at the water one more time and shivered. I imagined how much a belly flop would hurt from that high up. My legs were shaking. I took my shaky legs and walked back toward the ladder. The line started to move backward to let me down.

"Keats, you can do it," I heard the manny

yelling. He sounded like that gymnastics coach who cheered when the girl vaulted with a broken leg. The manny was standing there with his shirt on and all of our bags packed. Lulu, India, and Belly were standing next to him, looking up at me on the high dive.

Suddenly I turned around and ran as fast as I could to the end of the board. I leaped off and put my arms straight out like wings. I could feel everybody's eyes watching me. The air felt light, and everything was in slow motion. I felt like an angel. I hit the water and got the biggest wedgie of my life, but I pulled it out before I came to the surface.

When I came up out of the water, the manny fell to his knees and ripped his shirt off. He began whipping his shirt around in circles like he was Brandi Chastain, the soccer player who had done that after her team won the Women's World Cup. They show a clip of Brandi Chastain doing that every time there's a women's soccer game on television.

Sarah swam to me and told me that my jump was "fantastical *and* spectacular."

I climbed out of the pool and could feel my ears smiling, even though I was trying to pretend that it was no big deal.

The manny carried me out to the Eurovan on top of his shoulders like I had just made the winning home run of a baseball game. The kids at the pool stood by the chain-link fence and watched us until we were inside the Eurovan.

We got into the van, and the manny's cell phone rang. It was Mom. I tapped the manny on the shoulder and whispered, "Tell her I jumped off the high dive." He didn't.

They spoke quickly, and then he hung up.

"Your mom said that we should go celebrate by going out to dinner and then ice cream."

"I scream," said Belly, and she screamed.

Instead of ordering a vanilla cone, I ordered a banana split with whipped cream and nuts. The manny asked me to tell my jumping-off-the-diving-board story three times. By the third time I had decided that I knew I was going to jump the whole time and I just pretended to walk toward the ladder for dramatic effect.

Lulu rolled her eyes.

When we got home, I ran in to tell Grandma that I had finally jumped from the high dive. I started screaming the news even before I reached the living room.

"Grandma! You won't believe it. I jumped . . ."

I ran into the living room. Uncle Max, Mom,

and Dad were sitting on the couch. Their eyes were red, and they had balled-up Kleenex in their hands.

Grandma's big, shiny hospital bed was gone. And so was Grandma.

August 16

Grandma died today.

I didn't get to tell her that I jumped off of the high dive.

24 "Somewhere over the Rainbow, Bluebirds Fly"

I'd never been to a funeral before. Nobody that I knew had ever died. I wore my suit, the same one that I had worn out to dinner with Grandma in New York City. There was still a Balthazar matchbook in the coat pocket. I held on to it during the memorial service.

Grandma's funeral wasn't like the funerals that I've seen on television. On television people sob uncontrollably and yell, "Why? Why?" Mom watched a movie on Lifetime once where a woman threw herself onto the casket and had to be dragged away by her teenage children. The next week, in a different movie, the same woman was trying to find her kidnapped child. She had a very traumatic life. I don't know exactly what *traumatic* means, but I think it's what makes dark circles underneath your eyes, like the ones Mom had the first year of Belly's life.

Instead of a casket Grandma had an urn. She had been cremated, which meant that her body had been burned, so that she was now ash. She had told Mom that she didn't want to take up space after she died. Instead she wanted to be thrown into the wind so that she could "dance forever around the world."

Uncle Max stood up at the service and talked about how much fun Grandma had been. He said that one time when he and Mom were little, Grandma had chased them all over the house and even outside, pretending like she was going to put them in the basement. I looked over at Mom, and she winked at me through the tears in her eyes. Uncle Max and Mom had locked Grandma out of the house and jumped for joy because they had won the game. Grandma surprised them by punching a hole through the screen door with her fist and letting herself in. They stood in disbelief, and Grandma grabbed them and tickled them until Uncle Max peed his pants.

Grandma's canasta friends were sitting behind us. They laughed at the story. I could hear June's chuckle turn into a cough. I turned around, and she mouthed "Hi" to me and blew her nose with an embroidered linen hanky, the kind you put in the washing machine when you're done instead of throwing it away.

When Uncle Max was done with his story, he

came back over to sit with us. He sat next to the manny in the row in front of me. When Uncle Max sat down, the manny put his arm around him, with his hand on his shoulder. Uncle Max dropped his head into his hands, and his back started to move up and down. The manny rubbed his shoulder.

I started to cry when I saw Uncle Max cry.

Lulu held my hand.

I looked over at India, who was holding Belly on her lap. India was wearing the pearl necklace that Grandma had given her.

Three more people stood up and told funny stories about Grandma. The time she changed clothes in the back of a cab in Las Vegas. The time she ordered a pizza because there was a spider in her bathtub and she needed somebody to kill it. The time a ballpoint pen poked through her purse and she didn't know it. She walked around the mall for an hour and a half while the pen drew a big blue spot on the back of her white pants, right on her bottom. She went around the rest of the day asking strangers, "Does this big blue dot make my butt look big?"

I didn't know that there could be so much laughing at a funeral. Dad said it was because Grandma had laughed so much in her own life.

June got up and said that Grandma had told her that some of the happiest times of her life had been in our living room this summer.

June said, "She had everything that she wanted. A garden. Opera music. And her grandchildren."

The manny looked back at me and smiled. His eyes were red, and I could tell that he had been crying too.

I thought about Grandma's favorite opera, *La Bohème*, and the girl, Mimi, who died with people around her who loved her.

Grandma was like Mimi.

When all of the stories were done, Lulu played the piano and we all sang:

> "Somewhere over the rainbow,
> bluebirds fly. . . ."

On the way home from the funeral service Mom held the urn with Grandma's ashes in her lap. It was a fancy urn with gold trim and red jewels. It looked like if you rubbed it, a genie might pop out and grant wishes. I'd wish for Grandma to come back. The manny drove Uncle Max's Honda Accord behind us. Uncle Max sat in the passenger seat, and the manny had his right arm up with his hand on the back of Uncle Max's head. I watched them from the back window of the Eurovan.

Grandma's canasta friends came over to our house to eat the food that they had brought over the day before. India called it senior-citizen cuisine.

Deviled eggs. Pimento cheese sandwiches. Ambrosia.

I looked up *ambrosia* in the dictionary. It said that it was anything that looked or smelled delicious. The ambrosia that Grandma's canasta friends brought over should be called something else. It looked like the pink stomach medicine that Dad drinks out of the bottle during tax season. It smelled like Lulu's kiwi pectin shampoo-and-conditioner combination.

We ate in Grandma's garden. There was a light breeze that cooled off the sunny, hot day.

Belly sat on June's lap and put both hands on June's round cheeks. She squeezed her face so that June's lips stuck out and she looked like a puffer fish.

Belly said, "Are you an Oompa Loompa?"

Belly meant this as a compliment, because she loves the Oompa Loompas from *Willy Wonka and the Chocolate Factory*.

Lulu gasped, "Belly!"

It didn't bother June. She didn't know what an Oompa Loompa was.

Grandma's canasta friends hugged us and said that we were in their thoughts. Thelma and Wanda argued over who would drive home. They had bought a new red Audi convertible together. Thelma won the argument, and they drove away listening to Vivaldi.

Grandma liked Vivaldi.

Violet carried her pie plates and walked home with Virginia, who had an unlit cigarette dangling from her mouth.

June was the last to leave. Mom had given her Grandma's canasta cards, the ones that had Grandma's initials engraved on them. June held them in her fat hands and kissed Belly good-bye.

June said, "She was my best friend, you know. The most interesting person I've ever met." Then she left.

Be interesting, I thought to myself.

After everyone had left, the manny put "Quando Men Vo" on the CD player. It was Grandma's favorite song from *La Bohème*. We stood in the garden, and Mom and Uncle Max opened Grandma's urn and tossed her ashes into the breeze. They blew all around us; some landed on the hydrangea bush, and a piece landed on my forehead. Belly spun around in circles, looking up into the sky, which was dusted with ash. Dad was on his back looking straight up into the air. India and Lulu were lying beside him.

Nobody said anything.

We just watched Grandma begin her dance around the world.

August 19

We watched Grandma's ashes blow across the garden. I thought I would be really sad, but instead it was kind of exciting. It gave me that same feeling that I get when the barber uses the electric razor to clip the back of my neck. Like I had an imaginary crown on.

When I went out into the living room to put one of Grandma's garden books on the feng shui coffee table, Belly was lying on her back on the floor where Grandma's bed had been. She looked like she was trying to catch the air with her arms. I asked her what she was doing, and she said that she was hugging Grandma. I believe her.

Born on this day: Malcolm Forbes, Bill Clinton, Coco Chanel

In the middle of the night I sneaked out of my room to get a glass of cranberry juice. On my way back through the living room I winked at Grandma.

25 I Teach the Children Only Good Things

It's Labor Day weekend, and there are only a few more days of summer vacation left. School begins on Tuesday. I was hoping to get a brand-new teacher who had never even heard of Lulu, but instead I was placed in Mrs. House's class. Mrs. House was Lulu's teacher in fourth grade. I met Mrs. House when Mom took me to back-to-school orientation. She was nice. I tried to get on her good side by admiring her white shoes and asking if they were made by Jimmy Choo. I don't know who Jimmy Choo is, but I do know that the lady who won the Oscar for Best Supporting Actress last year wore a pair of Jimmy Choo shoes with her vintage Valentino dress. I read it in an issue of *In Style* magazine that Lulu had stolen from the doctor's office.

Mrs. House told me that her shoes were Hush Puppies.

I tried to peek into Mrs. House's supply closet

to see if there was a Lulu shelf, but Mom caught me and grabbed me by the arm.

The manny keeps pretending to forget my teacher's name. He calls her Brick House. Like from the song.

He said, "I heard she's mighty, mighty and she lets it all hang out."

"'Shake it down, shake it down now,'" I said back.

Mom and the manny took us back-to-school shopping at the mall. I wanted to go to Saks Fifth Avenue, but Mom said that Saks Fifth Avenue was for special occasions and the fourth grade wasn't considered a special occasion.

I said to her, "Just remember, I can do all sorts of things at school that will make Mrs. House question your ability as a mother. Write on the desk. Paint my face during art class. Accidentally call her Mom."

Mom said, "That's so funny I forgot to laugh."

Lulu thinks that she's grown up now and talked Mom into buying her a miniskirt. She picked the ugliest color. It is the same color as lima beans. India bought fabric to make a hooded shawl out of. Belly bought an Orange Julius at the food court. She took three sips and then dropped it. It splashed on the shoes of a guy with a mall security jacket on. Mom apologized, but he still kept one hand on his regulation club hanging from his belt until we had the mess cleaned up.

It got Mom flustered.

Ms. Grant got flustered last year when we finished reading *Charlotte's Web* in class. She asked us if we thought Charlotte was heroic. The girl with the poofy red hair raised her hand and asked if Charlotte was the spider or the pig. Ms. Grant gave us a writing assignment and put her head down on her desk to rest. I think she fell asleep, because when she lifted her head, there were creases across her hot red cheeks.

When Mom finished cleaning up Belly's mess, we looked for new jeans for me. I couldn't find any jeans that fit me right. We tried the Gap, but they didn't carry a size small enough for me. The saleslady said, "Sorry, maybe you should try BabyGap."

I wanted to push her into a pile of perfectly folded sweaters.

I ended up having to get a pair of jeans that looked like they were made for first graders or kindergarteners. They were stiff dark blue denim and had golden yellow stitching. On the back right pocket were embroidered the words SMARTY PANTS. When I put them on, I looked like

Uncle Max's junior high pictures, like I was one of the Brady kids. I hated the jeans, but they were the only ones that we could find that fit me.

I bet Saks Fifth Avenue would have the perfect jeans.

At the shoe store Lulu bought shoes that were made out of rubber and made her as tall as Mom. India got a pair of black boots that were made in Italy. Belly got a shoehorn. She didn't know what it was, but she cried until Mom finally bought it.

I took my shoe off and put my foot on the cold metal thing that measures your foot. The shoe salesman adjusted it, and I pushed my heel forward, trying to make my foot seem bigger.

"Keep the heel pressed on the back," the salesman grumbled.

My foot had grown a whole size since the beginning of third grade. Even without pressing my heel forward! The bigger your feet are, the more choices that you have in shoes!

The manny picked up a pair of brand-new brown penny loafers and waved them in the air for me to see. They were dark suede and had slots on the top to put pennies in. The salesman went to the back and brought a pair out in my size. They were a little big, but I pretended that they weren't. Mom let me get them. The manny pulled two shiny pennies from his pocket and bent down and put them in the slots of my shoes.

I wore my new shoes for the rest of our shopping day. I put my old shoes in the shopping bag, and the manny carried it. My penny loafers made me feel grown up. They made me look like a lawyer out with his family, even though I needed to get back to the office, roll my sleeves up, and talk to my secretary through the intercom. I walked around the rest of the day with my hands in my front pockets. Whenever we stopped in a store, I leaned against the wall and crossed my feet like the models in the Brooks Brothers catalog. I just stared at the pennies in my shoes while everyone else shopped.

The manny told other people that I was his colleague. A colleague is somebody that you work with or that you are friends with. I learned it from Sarah's mom. She always calls me Sarah's colleague.

A saleslady asked me, "Are you waiting for your mother and sisters?"

"Yes. You know what a dangerous combination women and credit cards are," I said, trying to sound as old as I felt.

The saleslady laughed and said I was cute.

Penny loafers were not cute. I had to say something grown up.

I said, "Thanks, toots."

I had heard somebody say it on television once. A guy dressed in a fancy suit said it to a woman with a feathery hat who served him a drink with an olive in it.

The saleslady laughed again.

Mom turned to the manny and said, "Did you teach him that?"

The manny said, "No. I teach the children only good things."

Then he laughed.

I looked over to see if Lulu had heard him, but she didn't. She was looking at fake leather pants. She wants a pair, but Mom says she's too young for leather pants. Even fake ones.

Mom laughed at the manny too. She knew that the manny taught us all kinds of things. A few weeks before, when Mom and Dad were out to dinner, the manny had come over to make enchiladas and watch movies with us. We were on the couch, and an awful smell came drifting up from the floor in front of us. India and Lulu plugged their nose and squealed, "Ewww." I held my nose and pretended to gag. The manny held his nose and pointed at the dog.

He said, "Oh, gross. Housman squeezed a greaser."

"Housman squeezed a greaser. Housman squeezed a greaser," we all chanted.

A few days later Mom took Belly to the beauty shop because Belly wanted a pixie haircut like her friend Analise. When the lady who cut Belly's hair walked across the linoleum floor, her shoe made a squeaking noise.

Belly held her nose and yelled, "You squeezed a greaser. You squeezed a greaser."

Mom acted like she had no idea where Belly had learned it, but I think she suspected the manny.

Mom hasn't been back to that beauty shop since.

When we were done with our shopping, we rested in the food court. Belly had a chocolate-chip cookie with frosting. Lulu and India split a Cinnabon. The manny and I had lemonade from the place where they wear the funny red-blue-and-yellow hats that are too tall for their heads.

After sitting for a while, we gathered all the bags and walked toward the car. The sun was hot on the new, sticky black pavement, and it felt like we were parked miles away. When we saw the car, Lulu and I started to run as fast as we could to it.

"I get the backward seat by the window," I yelled.

"No. I do. It's the privilege that comes with being the oldest. Like becoming queen," Lulu yelled back.

"Firstborn *son* always gets to be king!" I screamed.

I had trouble running my fastest because I was in my new penny loafers that were a little too big. I was almost catching up to her when I tripped over the toe of my shoe and skidded across the pavement. Lulu didn't even stop to help. She kept running and yelled, "I won, I won," when she reached the car.

It didn't hurt.

I stood up and started to pick the tar off my elbow. There was also a tar stain across my shirt. I didn't care. It was India's hand-me-down Krispy Kreme T-shirt. I looked down at my penny loafers, and there was a big tar spot on the toe of my left shoe, and the penny was lying on the pavement, stained black and sticky.

That's when I started to cry.

I couldn't help it.

Mom and the manny thought my elbow hurt. I went with it. I grabbed my elbow and kept sobbing.

Lulu still got the good seat, but I could tell she felt guilty.

She grabbed my shoe and started to clean off the tar.

September 1

I got new penny loafers, but I think I'll keep nickels in them instead. I like silver better than copper. My foot is a whole size bigger since last year.

Mom and the manny rode in the front seats of the Eurovan. They laughed and talked. I think that's what Sarah and I will be like when we grow up. I tried to listen to see what they were talking about, but Lulu wouldn't stop singing to the radio. All I could hear was Mom telling an Uncle Max story and the manny calling someone cute. I bet it wasn't Lulu.

Born on this day: Rocky Marciano, Lily Tomlin, Gloria Estefan

The night before the first day of school the manny and Uncle Max came over to help us pick out our clothes for the next day. Lulu modeled her rubber shoes and miniskirt with a pink collared shirt. India modeled faded jeans and a multi-colored shirt. She kind of looked like a roll of Life Savers, but in a good way. I modeled my penny loafers and my SMARTY PANTS jeans, which I told them I hated because of those stupid words. I also had on a white button-down shirt and a blazer. Uncle Max said that I looked a little too eager to be at school. The manny said that maybe I shouldn't wear the blazer. He showed me how to unbutton my shirt a few buttons and roll up my sleeves. He called it relaxed chic. He told me that if I untucked my shirt, nobody would see that my jeans said SMARTY PANTS. Uncle Max showed me how to put gel in my hair, starting from the back and working forward.

Belly modeled her shoehorn. She walked through the living room like a runway model with nothing on except a shoehorn balanced on top of her head. She twirled around with her hands on her hips. Lulu grabbed a blanket and wrapped it around Belly.

Lulu hates naked people.

I showed the manny and Uncle Max all of my school supplies. The red plastic box that I had chosen to hold my pencils and erasers. The red plastic ruler. The battery-operated paper shredder that Mom let me get.

The manny helped me fit it all into the sleek black backpack that he had helped me pick out. He said that it looked just like the one he had seen in the Prada store. It looks just like the bag that I saw the hip and trendy people in business suits carrying in New York City.

I got my bag at Target.

Mom made us all take baths and wash our hair. She even cleaned out our ears with Q-tips. She said she was cleaning out the summer sand.

I hung my new outfit on my clothes valet and put my pocket change and watch in the bowl on top. I grabbed the BE INTERESTING coconut and rubbed it.

As I tried to fall asleep, I could hear Uncle Max and the manny downstairs packing our lunches and laughing. They sounded like Mom and Dad when I can hear them talking and laughing through my bedroom wall.

September 3

Tomorrow is the first day of school. Sarah and Scotty are in my class. I hope that Craig isn't.

I didn't grow very much this summer. Belly did. She wears the jeans that I wore in the first grade, and she's only three.

I heard Uncle Max ask Mom and Dad if they wanted to have dinner with the manny and him on Friday night at the fancy restaurant. I want to go, but Dad said no when I asked. I think they want to talk about adult things, like who's sexy in Hollywood and how much houses cost. I wonder who will stay with us. Grandma used to when the manny couldn't.

Born on this day: Memphis Slim, Alan Ladd, Marguerite Higgins

27 Dumb Butt

I woke up early the next morning and put on my school clothes that were hanging, clean and ironed, on the clothes valet. I kept my white dress shirt untucked just like the manny had showed me, because I didn't want anybody to see that the back of my jeans said SMARTY PANTS. I slipped on my penny loafers, which had shiny nickels stuck in the slots, and I bolted down the steps. When I ran through the living room, I winked at Grandma. I imagined her saying, "Take me wherever you're going, handsome." Or maybe she really did say it.

Lulu and India were already having breakfast when I ran into the kitchen. Lulu's hair had big curls in it. She looked like Nellie Oleson, the mean girl from *Little House on the Prairie*. I watch *Little House on the Prairie* reruns on channel 36. India had little braids all around her head. She looked like Sarah did when she got back from the Caribbean last spring break.

"You sure are excited for school," Mom said.

"He thinks his teacher is foxy," Lulu said, grinning.

"How are things down at Oleson's Mercantile?" I asked her, and pulled on one of her curls.

Mom laughed. She loved *Little House on the Prairie* when she was little.

We ate breakfast quickly so we wouldn't miss the bus. Mom handed us our lunches, and we raced out the door. I didn't run because I didn't want to fall again and stain my shoes. I just walked fast, like the grandmothers who walk around the mall.

At school Mrs. House asked how Lulu was doing.

I answered, "She still has that Tai Pei personality."

I'm not quite sure what a Tai Pei personality is, but I heard Dad say that Lulu inherited her Tai Pei personality from him.

Mrs. House looked at me like I was speaking Chinese. Then she said, "Keats, would you pass out these lists of classroom rules to everybody?"

I made sure that the back of my pants was covered and walked to the front of the classroom.

Rule number one was "Be nice." It was written in black marker and had a big yellow smiley face next to it. Craig was in my class. When I put a sheet of rules on top of his desk, he pretended to knock it off accidentally with his elbow. I bent over, picked it up, and put it back on his desk.

"Thanks, smarty-pants," he said.

I flared my nostrils and pointed to rule number one on the sheet on his desk.

"I *said* thanks," he said.

I didn't waste any more time with him. How could I expect polite behavior from someone who didn't even know what a verb was? Last year Ms. Grant called on Craig and asked him to explain what a verb was. He stood up and said that a verb was when you burped and a little bit of vomit came up into your mouth.

He wasn't trying to be funny.

I could have given Ms. Grant the correct answer, if only the poofy-red-haired girl hadn't conditioned and curled her hair the night before.

I passed the rest of the rules out. When I got to Sarah's desk, she told me that she liked my shoes. She said that her dad had shoes like that and her mom said that they were "smart."

When I walked back to Mrs. House's desk to return the rest of the papers, she extended her foot out and said, "Look, I wore the shoes that you like so much."

Mrs. House wiggled her foot and asked if I

would be line leader on the way to lunch. I looked at Mrs. House's Hush Puppies and smiled while we were walking to lunch.

I told Sarah that the manny and Uncle Max had made my lunch. She wanted to trade with me before she even knew what was inside. I opened it and found a bag with five sushi rolls in it. Uncle Max learned how to roll sushi when he visited his college roommate in Japan last year. He rolled vegetables and rice inside little seaweed strips. Vegetable rolls are my favorite.

Taped to the bag of vegetable rolls was a two-dollar bill that had a note written across it: BE WHO YOU ARE. WE LOVE YOU. THE MANNY AND UNCLE MAX.

I put it in the back pocket of my SMARTY PANTS.

In the classroom that afternoon Craig bent down by his desk and said, "Look, I found a nickel."

I looked down at my shoes. My right penny loafer still had a nickel in the slot, but the left one was empty. I didn't say anything. I thought maybe Craig needed the nickel more than I did. Maybe he could use it as a down payment for a better personality. I pulled the two-dollar bill out of my pocket and read, "Be who you are."

I kept it on my desk while I wrote my essay titled "What I Did This Summer." I wrote about

Grandma and the garden. I wrote about her funeral and how we watched her ashes dance around the garden. I also wrote about being brave enough to jump off the high dive. I turned it in and started to work on my math review assignment. An hour later Mrs. House called me to her desk to pick up my graded essay.

She said, "You're a very descriptive writer. May I keep this essay to read to next year's class as an example?"

I nodded yes and imagined Mrs. House devoting a whole shelf in her closet to my projects.

Then she said, "It's nice to read an essay that is about important things that happen."

Then she stood up and cleared her throat to get the class's attention.

"This essay was written by Keats, and it's an example of thoughtful writing." Then she read my essay to the class. Craig pretended to be sleeping with his head on his desk.

The class clapped when Mrs. House was finished, and Craig pretended that it had surprised him awake. He looked around like he was wondering what he had missed. He's a bad actor. I know he heard it.

The bell rang and Mrs. House dismissed us.

When I was getting on the bus, Craig said, "Bye, smarty-pants."

I wanted to scream at him and accuse him of stealing my nickel, but instead I said back to him, "See you tomorrow."

The manny met the bus. He wasn't doing anything strange. He was just standing there like a normal person. He hugged me when I got off the bus. When he turned to hug India, I noticed the words DUMB BUTT stitched across the back of his jeans pocket with yellow yarn. He didn't have his shirt untucked like he had shown me.

September 4

Today was the first day of school.

Craig is in my class, and he's already being mean to me, just like last year. I'm trying to remember what the manny said about not letting him bother me, but it's really hard. At recess he and his two friends said that they needed to have their first MASK meeting of the year. Sarah had her first meeting too. There were twelve kids on top of the monkey bars with her. I went to my spot behind the Dumpster and found where I had written my name on it, but somebody had added to it. Now it said, "Keats Dalinger . . . crys back here evry day." I thought that it must be Craig because *cries* and *every* were spelled wrong.

I didn't cry. I changed the *c* in *crys* to a *t*, so

that it said, "Keats Dalinger . . . trys back here evry day."

When I got home, the manny helped me pull the SMARTY PANTS stitching out of my back pocket. He took an old Levi's label from one of Dad's pairs of jeans and sewed it onto my jeans. He says next year he's going to be a fashion designer.

Born on this day: Beyoncé Knowles, Paul Harvey, Daniel Burnham

On Friday, Mom and Dad went out to dinner with Uncle Max and the manny. A high school girl named Amanda came over to watch us. She put braids in India's hair and painted Belly's toenails pink. Belly rubbed most of the nail polish off her toes and onto Housman's fur. Housman didn't mind. He thought she was petting him.

Lulu pretended that she and Amanda were the same age. She asked Amanda about boys and things like that.

Amanda told her, "The way to get a boy's attention is to be really dramatic and cry a lot. Make sure that the boy knows that you can't live without him by writing him love notes. If he still doesn't pay attention to you, write your first name on your notebook with his last name right after it. Boys love it when they think you want to marry them."

India looked at Amanda and asked, "Do you have a boyfriend?"

"No," Amanda said.

"Hmm," said India.

Amanda made popcorn and put on a movie that she had rented. It was called *Ever After*, and everybody talked with a snotty accent. Amanda and Lulu cried during it. I thought it was boring. I waited by the window for Mom and Dad's headlights to appear in the driveway.

While I waited, I started my own "Amanda Files" but only got as far as the title.

When Mom and Dad did get home, Lulu said, "Amanda's a lot more competent than the manny. Can she come watch us again sometime?"

I wanted to shove a pillow in Lulu's mouth.

"We'll see," said Dad, picking up Belly, who was sleeping on the couch.

Belly started laughing. She always pretends to be asleep when Mom and Dad come home from somewhere, and she always laughs when Dad picks her up.

"What do you think, Keats, should Amanda come back?" asked Mom.

I wanted to say, "No, she should move to New York City and write tragic romance movies for Lifetime," but Amanda was standing right next to me.

Instead I just nodded an unenthusiastic yes

and went to my bedroom to write in my journal.

September 7

I think the fourth grade is going to be just like the third grade. We had to write haiku in class today, and Mrs. House read one by one of her former students. It went like this:

> Be strong, healthy girl
> Belong only to yourself
> Beautiful woman.

I knew that it was Lulu's haiku even before Mrs. House told us. Mrs. House has a whole file in her drawer full of Lulu's drawings, poems, and papers.

Every time I ask to go to the bathroom, Craig asks if he can go and get a drink. He follows me and kicks my heels. He took my glasses and held them over the toilet like he was going to drop them in, but Mr. Robbins, a second-grade teacher, walked in. Craig pretended that I had dropped them, and handed my glasses back to me, saying, "Here you go, Keats." I'm not going to go to the bathroom at school anymore. I'll hold it all day until I get home.

At dinner tonight Lulu wouldn't stop talking

about Amanda. She acted like a movie star had come over to watch us. She even asked Dad if he thought that she looked a little bit like Julia Roberts. Dad loves Julia Roberts.

Born on this day: Grandma Moses, Queen Elizabeth I, Buddy Holly

We'll Always Be Good Friends, No Matter What

I woke up on Saturday morning and found a memorandum attached to my door with Scotch tape. It called a family trial to "investigate collected evidence." It was from Lulu. They were taped on all of our bedroom doors. Even Belly had one, but she shredded it in the battery-operated paper shredder that I'd gotten with school supplies.

Family trials are called only when something is really important to a member of the family. If a family trial is called, it means that Mom and Dad will really listen and try to change whatever the problem is. That's why I was worried. The only evidence Lulu had been collecting was about the manny.

We have had only two other family trials. One was about the need for another bathroom. Lulu called that trial. The other trial was called by Dad. It was about not leaving our toys in the driveway. He had backed his car out of the garage and felt a crunch underneath the tire. He panicked because he thought it was Housman, but it was just Belly's Sit'n Spin. It doesn't spin anymore, so Belly just gets on it and sits.

After breakfast we all sat in the living room for family court. Lulu sat at the coffee table and opened up a three-ring binder in front of her. It was full of marked-up papers with lists on them. Lulu was wearing a blazer and had her hair pulled up so that she looked like a lawyer.

It was "The Manny Files."

She began stating her case. "I have brought forth this lawsuit because I think it's time that we had a normal babysitter again, like Amanda. I'm not sure that the manny is a good influence on young, impressionable minds like Belly's, Keats's, and India's."

India rolled her eyes and crossed her arms. She didn't say anything because we're not allowed to interrupt in family court. A person is allowed to have his or her say. We're not allowed to roll our eyes, either.

Lulu said, "I'll hold you in contempt of court, India."

In family court being in contempt means you have to unload the dishwasher that night after dinner. I was held in contempt at the last trial because I shot a rubber band at Lulu while she was making her case for having an additional bathroom put in for her. She said that I never put the toilet seat up when I used it and that it was disgusting. I always put the toilet seat up. It's Housman that gets the seat wet when he drinks from the toilet, which he's not supposed to do. We didn't get a new bathroom. Instead we got a laminated "Bathroom Rules" list, which hangs next to the light switch.

1. Flush the toilet when you are finished.
2. Close the lid when you are finished.
3. Clean up after yourself.
4. If you stand up to pee, make sure the seat is up.

(That one is for me.)

5. Keep out of Lulu's drawer.

The last rule is written in black marker in Lulu's handwriting.

India sat up, and Lulu started to list all of the evidence that she'd been recording since the manny arrived. My stomach hurt even before she started reading her files. I knew Mom and

Dad liked the manny, but what if they agreed with Lulu that some of the stuff he let us do was inappropriate?

"Evidence number one: He lets Belly roll in the mud down by the river, teaching Belly that it's okay to get dirty."

Mom smirked but stopped when Lulu looked at her, because she was afraid that Lulu would hold her in contempt. Mom hates unloading the dishwasher.

"Evidence number two: Whenever I see a boy that I know out in public, he sings 'I'm in the Mood for Love.'"

Dad coughed, but I think he was stifling a giggle. Not bad so far. Everything would be fine as long as Lulu didn't bring up the time we had a picnic on the roof of the house. Mom and Dad might not like that one.

Lulu looked down at her notebook again and pointed to something at the bottom of the page.

"Evidence number three: The other morning he chased after the bus and barked with the rest of the dogs from around town. The bus driver was laughing so hard that it put every child's life in danger on that bus."

Dad started cough-laughing again.

"This isn't funny," said Lulu, glaring. "We're talking about the future of *your* children."

Dad stopped coughing, but his ears still smiled. They were red.

Mom wasn't laughing, which worried me. Had Lulu made her point? If she had, the manny might be joining Amy in the Nannies Lulu's Fired Club.

Mom said, "You're right, sweetie. If this is really a concern of yours, then we will listen. We want you to feel safe and happy."

I hated hearing Mom say that. It made me feel like throwing up. I felt safe and happy with the manny. I looked at India, but she didn't look like she was going to stand up and say anything in the manny's defense. Lulu is usually the only one who speaks at family meetings. India and I are scared of her, and Mom and Dad know it. They take us into a room and speak to us privately about how we can't let Lulu intimidate us. *Intimidate* is the word Mom uses. I think it means "to threaten with ugly faces." That's what Lulu does.

Lulu continued reading "The Manny Files" on and on and on, and I held my breath, hoping that she wouldn't mention the time the manny let me use the women's restroom at the gas station because the men's smelled bad. Mom might not like that.

As Lulu read, I remembered why I liked the

manny so much. I had forgotten some of the fun things that had happened since we met him. Jumping on the trampoline. Running through the sprinklers at the golf course in our clothes. Writing JUST MARRIED on the back window of the Eurovan in shoe polish to see who would honk at us.

While Lulu read, I watched Mom and Dad to see if they thought Lulu had some good points. They nodded their heads like they were agreeing with her. Sometimes I nod my head like I'm agreeing with her even when I'm not. It makes her stop talking. I hoped that's what they were doing.

I thought about Amy, the nanny that Lulu got fired. I don't remember her, but I think that I would probably have liked her, since Lulu didn't.

Then I thought about how I'd pack my carry-on luggage, the one with wheels, and sneak into the back of the manny's car if he had to leave. I wondered if the manny and Uncle Max would still be friends, or if the manny would have to go to jail because of the time he stole the neighbor's newspaper so I could cut out an article for "Current Events." We returned it to our neighbor's yard. It just had a hole in it where an article about political morality had been.

When Lulu was finished reading the last page

of "The Manny Files," Mom and Dad asked if India, Belly, or I had anything to add. Belly was staring at the palms of her hands like she had never noticed them before. India scooted back on the couch and let out a big sigh. I could tell she was too flustered to speak. I looked at Lulu. I looked at my parents. I looked at Lulu again. She glared at me. And this time I glared right back.

"I *love* the manny!" I finally squealed, but then I didn't want to make Dad jealous, so I pointed to him said, "He reminds me of you because he's funny and smart." I couldn't believe I was talking at a family trial. And neither could Lulu. She stood there shocked, with her mouth open.

I went on, "I think he's the best nanny we've ever had, and not just because he does crazy things. India and Belly like him. Uncle Max likes him. The teachers at school like him. The bus drivers like him. Grandma liked him."

That's when I started to cry. Not the kind of cry that I used to do behind the Dumpster, or even the kind of cry that I did at Grandma's funeral, but a sobbing that I couldn't stop.

I went on through sobs, "The only one that doesn't like him is Lulu, and that's only because he doesn't let her boss him around." I thought this would be a good time to pound the table like I'd seen the lawyers do on television. It startled Belly, who stopped looking at her hands and said, "The manny's funny!" and she laughed a big fake laugh. "I love him."

Lulu glared at Belly, but Belly has never been intimidated by Lulu, and she kept laughing. Then Lulu steered her glare toward me.

"The only reason you like the manny is because he makes *my* life miserable!" she screamed.

The trial had gotten out of control, and Mom and Dad knew it. Mom held Lulu by the shoulders and said that she and Dad needed some time to deliberate their verdict and that they'd seriously think on it for the rest of the weekend.

Maybe the weekend was all I needed to convince them that the manny should stay and it was Lulu who needed to leave.

Lulu looked very pleased with herself, as if her last outburst would determine what the verdict would be. India chewed on her nails. Belly held Housman, who was wrapped in a blanket, in her arms like a newborn baby. She didn't really know what was going on.

The meeting was adjourned, and I ran to Dad's office to call the manny on his cellular phone to tell him what had happened. I know his number in case of an emergency. This was definitely an emergency. He picked up after the third ring. I remembered he once told India to let the phone ring at least three times so that she didn't seem eager and lonely.

When he answered, I whispered because talking about family court outside of family court is forbidden.

I whispered, "Hi. It's Keats."

"Is everything all right?" He sounded worried. Then I heard him say, "It's Keats," to someone who was with him.

I whispered some more. "We just had a family meeting about you. Lulu wants Mom and Dad to fire you and hire Amanda. Mom and Dad are thinking about it until the end of the weekend. What if they decide to fire you? I'll never see you again."

I started to cry again, but not the uncontrollable sobs from before.

The manny said, "Keats, even if they decide to hire Amanda, it doesn't mean that you'd never see me again. We'll always be good friends, no matter what. You'll see me all the time. I'll pick you up from school. We'll go to movies. We'll short-sheet Lulu's bed."

"But what about next year?" I said through my tears.

"What do you mean?" asked the manny.

"Next year and the cookbook and personal shopping and Cirque du Soleil!" I sniffled.

"My plans have changed. I thought I was going to leave, but I'm having too much fun here. I've made too many new friends that I want to be with, including you. Cirque du Soleil called and said I was too handsome to put in a costume anyway."

I laughed.

Then the manny said, "Your parents will make the right decision, even if it means that Amanda takes my place. Don't worry about it. I will always be around. Lulu can't do anything about that."

"Okay," I said, but I didn't mean it. I didn't think the manny understood Lulu's power. Amy disappeared for good. We never saw *her* again.

"By the way, your uncle Max says hello. We're getting ready to go to the grocery store." The manny said good-bye and hung up. I did feel a little better knowing that the manny and Uncle Max were still friends. I bet they raced grocery carts at the store.

That afternoon I worked on my math homework on the kitchen table.

Mom came in and said, "I've never seen you do your homework on a Saturday before. What's gotten into you?"

I said, "The manny says that education is the most important thing in a person's life and that it will take me wherever I want to go."

The manny never really said this, but I knew that Mom could never fire someone who got me to do my homework on my own without being asked six times and bribed with snacks. Especially on a Saturday.

"Oh," Mom said, and opened the cupboard and pulled out a bag of chocolate chips. "Do you want to help me make chocolate chip cookies?"

I answered, "No, thank you. The manny says that I should cut back on sugar."

He never said this, either, but I was on a roll.

I excused myself from the table and told Mom that if she needed me, I'd be in the bathroom flossing and brushing my teeth.

"In the middle of the day?" Mom asked.

"It's good hygiene," I said. "Haven't you noticed how white the manny's teeth are?"

Mom's a sucker for good hygiene.

Before dinner that night I helped Belly wash her hands in the kitchen sink. When Dad walked by, I said, "Good girl, Belly. Wash all the germs away, like the manny showed us."

Dad's a sucker for washing germs away.

Belly said, "I love the manny."

Nice touch, Belly.

That night I cried while I wrote in my journal. It wasn't a sad cry. It was a mad cry.

September 8

I'll never forgive Lulu if the manny has to leave. I'll never talk to her again as long as I live. I'll run away to Uncle Max's house and live with him, and then Mom and Dad will be sorry that they listened to Lulu.

Born on this day: Patsy Cline, Peter Sellers, Pink

But He's the Best One 30
We've Ever Had

The next day was Sunday, the day Mom and Dad would deliver their verdict. When I walked down the hallway, I saw Lulu in her room rearranging her furniture. She moves her furniture around every few weeks just to change it up. Mom calls it "wrong shui."

I went down the stairs and heard India and Mom and Dad in the kitchen.

I heard India say, "But he's the best one we've ever had."

I think she was talking about the manny, but I'm not sure because they stopped talking when I walked into the kitchen.

I poured a bowl of cereal and waited for them to start talking again, so that I could join in, but they didn't. India left the table to go upstairs to help Belly get dressed for the day.

Once India was gone, Dad rubbed me on the back and said, "I'm proud of you for standing up for yourself during yesterday's family trial."

"Yeah," Mom said. "It was very passionate and real, and I couldn't believe Lulu's face."

"She doesn't scare me anymore," I said.

Just as I said this, Lulu came around the corner. I don't think she heard me, but she knew something was going on, because she didn't leave the room. My conversation with Mom and Dad was over. Lulu was there to intimidate. I may still be a little scared of her.

Dad stood up and squeezed my shoulder and told me to get ready for a family bicycle ride on the bike path. I jumped out of my chair and went toward the garage to find my helmet. When I passed Lulu, she followed me with her eyes without blinking. Maybe she did hear me.

That afternoon Mom, Dad, and Lulu rode bikes. Belly rode in a seat behind Dad's bike. India and I were on Rollerblades.

Lulu kept trying to talk to me, but I pretended that I couldn't hear her because of my helmet. Even when we stopped at the little sandwich hut for lunch, I kept my helmet on. I didn't even smile at her when she said I had gotten really good on my Rollerblades.

I usually love our family trips on the bike path, but today all I could think about was the verdict.

When we got home, I started to unload the dishwasher.

"Wow!" said Mom. "I didn't even ask."

I said, "The manny said that we should chip in and help because helping is what being a family is all about."

He really did say that.

India helped me unload.

Mom and Dad went into the other room. Lulu sat on the steps in between the rooms trying to hear what Mom and Dad were saying.

When we finished unloading the dishwasher, Dad called us into the living room for the verdict.

I put on my best sad face and sat on the couch right next to India, who also had a face on like she was one of the orphans in *Annie*.

Mom said, "Lulu, we had no idea that you were so unhappy about the manny being here."

Uh-oh, I thought, and I could see India move to the edge of her chair and start to protest. Mom put her hand on India's knee to stop her from starting.

Mom added, "Lulu, you are becoming a young woman, and maybe you do need someone who understands what that's like. I'll talk to Amanda and . . ." And I could feel the tears working their way to the surface of my eyes. My ears felt hot, and they throbbed like my heart-beat was in them. The manny was going to get fired. I jumped up and shouted, "No!" just as

Mom said, "see if she can come over every once in a while."

Dad motioned for me to sit back down, and I did. I didn't know what was going on. Amanda was going to come over every once in a while, but where did that leave the manny? Lulu's forehead was wrinkled up, and I could tell that she was just as confused as I was.

Then Mom said, "However, the manny is a wonderful addition to our family, and as much as you may disagree, you need to accept that he will be with us for a long time."

Mom's speech made me shake my legs with excitement like I was next in line for the Ferris wheel. India leaned back in her chair and smiled. Belly was asleep. She was using Housman as a pillow.

Lulu slammed her binder shut and said, "This isn't over. I'll keep recording the manny's misdeeds. Maybe the school counselor will see how serious this is."

Lulu grumbled and went to her room.

I jumped on Mom's and Dad's laps and gave them hugs. Dad covered his lap, like he always does when we jump around him. I jumped on his lap once and it really hurt him. He leaned over and had trouble breathing. I thought I had hit one of his lungs. I found out later what I'd really hit.

I raced down the hall and called the manny. I didn't bother whispering.

31 "We Go Together, Like Rama, Lama, Lama, Kadingy, Kadin-a-Dong"

The third week of school Lulu has her first school dance ever. The eighth graders always celebrate the beginning of the school year with a boy-girl dance. I imagined them doing the hand jive, like in *Grease*, but India told me that the boys just mostly stand against one side of the cafeteria while the girls stand against the other side.

It sounded boring to me.

The manny said that when he was in the eighth grade, they weren't allowed to have a dance because the town preacher didn't allow it. He said that nobody in the whole town was allowed to express themselves through choreography or dance freely until he fought it and they finally got to have a great big formal dance.

India said, "That wasn't you. That was Kevin Bacon in *Footloose*."

"Oh, yeah," said the manny. "I forgot."

Lulu wants Fletcher to dance with her at the

dance. She has been using Amanda's methods of getting a boy's attention. The first method was to cry around Fletcher. Lulu couldn't make herself cry. In fact, I don't know if she *can* cry. Instead she rubbed her eyes until they were red and then blew her nose like she'd been crying.

Fletcher said to her, "Don't get too close to me, I don't want to catch that cold."

Next she wrote him a love note. When she passed it across the classroom, it stopped on Jeremy's desk. He thought it was for him and opened it up and read it. After school Jeremy told Lulu that he was flattered but thought it was better that they just stayed friends.

As a last resort she wrote LULU WILLIAMS on the front of her notebook. Williams is Fletcher's last name. When he saw it, he called her a stalker and said that he was going to get a restraining order. I don't know what a restraining order is, but on the soap operas it's what they give someone who has crazy eyes, the same eyes Mom has when she chases us around the house.

The day that Fletcher told Lulu he was going to get a restraining order, she cried on the bus ride home. She *can* cry. She looked out the window so she wouldn't see the other kids staring at her. India told the other kids that Lulu was sad because her pet bird, Dorothy, had been eaten by a cat. Lulu doesn't even have a pet bird named Dorothy.

I've noticed that India sticks up for Lulu a lot.

When the bus stopped at our stop, the manny was doing one-armed push-ups on the sidewalk. The bus driver laughed and adjusted her pink neckerchief.

"Bye, darlin'," she said to Lulu. "I'm sorry about your bird."

We climbed off the bus. I gave the manny a high five.

Lulu walked way in front of us.

The manny could tell that something was wrong, so he didn't tease her.

"What's the matter with Lulu?" the manny asked India.

India told him the whole story. About Amanda's advice. About the school dance. About the restraining order.

When we got home, the manny walked upstairs to Lulu's room to see if he could help make her feel better. India and I put drinking glasses up against her door and listened. I used a martini glass. It didn't work very well, but I liked the shape.

"India told me what happened today. Do you want to talk about it?" the manny asked.

"Not to *you*," said Lulu. "You wouldn't understand what it's like to like a boy who doesn't like you back." She was still mad because family court hadn't gone her way.

"Maybe I can imagine," said the manny.

There was a long silence. Lulu probably wanted the manny to leave.

But he didn't.

Instead he said, "You know at the beginning of *Grease* when Sandy has a broken heart and doesn't understand why Danny is being such a jerk?"

"Yeah," Lulu said with a what's-your-point tone in her voice.

"Danny is being a jerk because he's afraid that his friends will think he's not cool if he's nice to Sandy. Then at the end when Sandy dresses in the tight black clothes and makes her hair wild, Danny notices her."

Lulu said, "I'm not wearing a strapless shirt and tight black Lycra pants to the dance."

"That's not what I mean," said the manny. "I think you should make Fletcher *want* your attention instead of trying so desperately to get his. It's called being unattainable. If you stop giving Fletcher attention, he'll miss it. The next thing you know, you'll be singing, 'We go together, like rama, lama, lama, kadingy, kading-a-dong'"

India and I giggled behind the closed door, and the manny and Lulu stopped talking.

We sat really still until Lulu finally said, "That makes sense, except for the part about the song. How do you know so much about boys?"

"It takes a lot of pain and learning to become this wise, Grasshopper," the manny said, pretending to be the master in *Kung Fu*.

It got quiet. I think Lulu gave the manny a hug. Either that or she smothered him with a pillow.

The door opened, and the manny and Lulu, who was holding his hand, looked down at India and me sitting on the floor.

"We were just having martinis," I said, holding up my glass.

Lulu pretended to be mad, but she still laughed.

She took the manny's advice and ignored Fletcher for the rest of the week.

The night of the dance India let Lulu borrow one of her Mexican blouses. Lulu wore her new miniskirt, and Mom curled her hair and even let her wear lipstick. Lulu pouted her lips out, even though the lipstick was clear gloss. It just looked like she had on Chap Stick.

Uncle Max and the manny came over to give

Lulu a ride to the dance on their way to dinner. I think they were celebrating something, because they were both dressed in suits. I ran to my room to get pocket squares for each of them to wear in the front pocket of their suit coat. Red for the manny. Blue for Uncle Max. I'd gotten the pocket squares at Mr. Henley's garage sale next door. A quarter apiece.

The manny adjusted Uncle Max's blue pocket square, then he licked his hand and patted down his cowlick.

When Lulu walked down the stairs, the manny said, "You look beautiful."

"Tell me about it, stud," said Lulu, pretending to be Olivia Newton-John in *Grease*.

She did look pretty.

As they were all walking out the door, Uncle Max said, "Lulu, be sure to call us if you need anything. A dance partner. An Altoid. More deodorant."

Lulu whirled around and yelled, "What*ever*!"

She hates the word *deodorant*.

Dad, India, and I worked on a jigsaw puzzle and waited for Lulu to return home. Mom worked on giving Belly a bath.

Lulu's friend Margo and her mom brought Lulu home from the dance. Uncle Max and the manny had come back from their dinner and were at our house waiting to hear how the dance went. They were playing Scrabble.

Lulu told them that she had had a great time and that she had mostly danced with all of her girlfriends. I asked her how they danced, and she said, "Like this," and started jumping straight up and down.

She told India that Fletcher had asked her if she was mad at him, because she didn't talk to him anymore. She had said she didn't know what he was talking about, and they had danced to a slow song. India made Lulu pretend that she was Fletcher and show her how they had danced. Lulu put her hands on India's hips, and India had her hands on Lulu's shoulders. They didn't move their feet, only their shoulders. Back and forth. Back and forth.

I thought, *Maybe Lulu should've taken dance lessons all of these years instead of piano lessons.*

The manny said, "Time for all children to go to bed."

Lulu, India, and I walked toward our bedrooms. Belly had already been in bed for an hour and a half.

The manny said, "Where are you going, Lulu? You need to stay out here with the adults and tell us more about the dance."

Lulu smiled at us. I could tell she was thinking, *Ha, ha.*

"Totally unfair," grumbled India as we pretended to go to bed. We really sat in the hallway and listened to Lulu's stories about the dance.

Margo had danced with a boy named D.J. They had played a Duran Duran song. Fletcher had burped in Lulu's ear while they were dancing.

That night Lulu officially dropped her lawsuit against the manny.

She put memorandums on our doors the next morning.

September 19

I think Lulu wants the manny to stay in our family for a while. She said that the manny knew how to give boy advice better than Amanda.

I can't wait until I'm old enough to go to dances. I don't want to dance with girls, though. I want to dance by myself, like I'm in a music video.

Born on this day: Dr. Amy Whittington, Sir William Golding, Adam West

32 D-i-g-n-i-d-y

The day after Lulu's dance I sat on the top of the monkey bars with Sarah during morning recess. I told her all of Lulu's dance stories. Sarah played with a yellow cottonwood leaf while I talked. I was just getting ready to tell her about Fletcher burping in Lulu's ear when a kickball hit me in the side of the head.

"Sorry," said Craig, but I don't think it was an accident.

He ran underneath the monkey bars, and just then Sarah's shoe flew off and hit him in the head.

"Sorry," said Sarah, but I don't think *that* was an accident either.

Craig rubbed his head and started to say something, when Mrs. House blew her whistle, which was our signal to line up to go inside. We hopped down, and Sarah put her shoe back on and winked at me.

When we got inside, Mrs. House reminded us that it was time for the spell-off to see who would represent our classroom in the all-school spelling bee. Lulu was in the spelling bee every year that she was in the elementary school, but she always got out in the first round. She always got words like *nauseous* and *discharge.* She couldn't spell them because she was gagging.

We all stood up at our desks, and Mrs. House went around the room giving us words to spell. If we misspelled them, we were out and we had to sit down. Craig was the first one out. He misspelled *manners.* He spelled it with one *n.* I bet he could have spelled *correctional facility* right.

We went around the room six times. My classmates were slowly eliminated and sat down at their desks. Sarah misspelled *psychedelic.* Elizabeth misspelled *precious.* Scotty misspelled *coupon.*

After seven rounds it was down to Sarah's friend Sage and me.

Mrs. House said, "Sage, your word is *dignity.*"

Sage started to spell. "D-i-g-n-i-d-y. *Dignity.*"

"Nope. I'm sorry, Sage. Keats, your word is *dignity.*"

I spelled, "D-i-g-n-i-t-y. *Dignity.*"

"That's correct, Keats. If you spell this next word correctly, you will represent our classroom at the all-school spelling bee on Friday. The word is *fantastic*."

I spelled it without even thinking. "F-a-n-t-a-s-t-i-c. *Fantastic*."

"Correct!" exclaimed Mrs. House.

The class cheered, except for Craig. He frowned at me.

September 20

I think if I do well in the all-school spelling bee, Mrs. House will finally stop introducing me to the other teachers as Lulu's little brother. Maybe she'll even put my picture up on her bulletin board or tell her class next year all about me. Maybe she'll have Belly in her class someday and she'll call her Keats's little sister.

The manny picked me up from school today. While I was waiting for him, Craig was throwing gravel from the playground up in the air. He pretended that it was an accident whenever the gravel landed on me like rain. It hurt, but I didn't cry. I think the manny saw us, because when I got into the car, he asked if everything was okay. I told him that Craig and I were just playing. I

don't want the manny to think I get picked on. I
want him to think that I'm cool.

Born on this day: Sister Kenny, Ferdinand "Jelly
Roll" Morton, Dr. Joyce Brothers

33 Skeet, Skeet, Skeet!

For the next week the manny picked out words from the dictionary to quiz me with.

Elegant. Chivalry. Flamboyant.

He picked the words that he liked.

When the manny was gone, Dad picked out words from the dictionary to quiz me with.

Portfolio. Dividends. Protocol.

He picked the words that he liked.

By the morning of the spelling bee, I knew how to spell everything from *adversity* to *zenith*.

I dressed in my loafers, blue jeans, and blue-and-white pin-striped button-down shirt and rolled up my sleeves. I slipped my navy sweater vest over it to make me look more serious. India spiked my hair. She said that I needed to look serious and playful, that's how the successful people look.

Donald Trump. Bill Gates. Ellen DeGeneres.

Mom, Dad, Uncle Max, and the manny came

to watch the spelling bee. They sat in the third row. The manny had GO KEATS written on his forehead in green Magic Marker, like he was at a football game. Kids from class recognized him from my school birthday party and pointed at him. Ms. Grant waved to him and smiled without showing her teeth, the kind of smile where you scrunch up your cheeks and smile with your eyes instead of your mouth.

The finalist from each classroom sat in a row of chairs that faced the student-filled bleachers. It was like we were the leaders of Spelling Congress. Mr. Allen, our principal, was the emcee. He straightened his toupee and introduced each one of us by our name and our classroom teacher.

Then we began.

Sophie, one of the first-grade representatives, was the first to spell. She missed her word, *trophy*. I expected her to cry, but she laughed and skipped into the bleachers and hugged her mother. That's what I wanted to do. If I missed my word, I wasn't going to cry. I was going to shrug my shoulders, hold my head up high, and go sit with my family. I hoped.

When it was my turn, I stood up so fast that my chair fell backward and slammed against the floor. The entire audience flinched like it was a gunshot, and then they started to giggle and laugh. Not a good start.

As I stepped up to the microphone, something came flying out of the crowd and landed right in front of Mr. Allen and me. It was my Scooby Doo underwear. The ones that had been missing since Craig stole them from the swimming pool locker room last May. The kids started laughing, and you could hear the rumble of moving feet in the bleachers. They sounded like the people in the movies who are at a town meeting and the mayor says something shocking about how the children are in danger of becoming delinquents.

I looked up into the crowd and saw Craig grinning with narrow eyes like the Wicked Witch of the West. I wanted to throw water on him and watch him melt into the ground. My ears burned and I could tell they were red. My nostrils flared like they do when I'm trying not to cry. I couldn't cry. It was one thing to cry behind a Dumpster, but to cry into a microphone in front of the whole school would make it impossible for me ever to come to school again. I thought about what the manny had told me about how to handle things like this.

I said into the microphone, "Wow. I didn't know I had such a fan base. This must be how the Rolling Stones feel."

The teachers and parents all rumbled with laughter. The kids looked confused, except Craig. He looked annoyed.

The manny gave me a thumbs-up sign. He crept down from the bleachers, grabbed my Scooby Doo underwear off the floor, and shoved them into his pocket. He returned to his seat next to Uncle Max.

Mr. Allen turned to me and said, "Your word is *magnificent.*"

"*Magnificent.* M-a-g-n-i-f-i-c-e-n-t. *Magnificent.*"

"Correct," said Mr. Allen, and the crowd cheered.

I went back to my seat and felt pleased with myself. So that's how Lulu felt.

The spelling bee went on for two hours. Kids sat down as they missed their words: *incorrect, anticlimax, disqualify.* I spelled all of my words correctly: *intense, prepared, prodigy.*

The last two people in the spelling bee were a fifth grader named Kyle and me.

Kyle stepped up to the microphone, and his class chanted for him. "Kyle, Kyle, Kyle!"

Mr. Allen gave him the word *harmonious* to spell.

Kyle accidentally spelled it *-eous* instead of *-ious.*

Kyle's class sighed in disappointment. He sat down in his chair, and I could tell from his face that he was chanting in his head, *Miss it. Miss it. Miss it.* If I misspelled the word, he still had a chance to win.

I stepped up to the microphone. Mr. Allen said, "Keats. The word is *harmonious.*"

Harmonious. H-a-r-m-o-n-i-o-u-s *Harmonious.*"

"Correct," said Mr. Allen as Kyle put his head in his hands. Mr. Allen went on, "If you spell this final word correctly, you will be our spelling-bee champion." My class chanted my name. "Keats, Keats, Keats!" Only it sounded like, "Skeet, Skeet, Skeet!" I really had to pee. I looked at the manny, and he mouthed, "You can do it," just like he had said at the swimming pool when I jumped off the high dive. I imagined Grandma chanting with them.

"Keats, Keats, Keats!"

Mr. Allen quieted the crowd and said, "Your word is *interesting.*"

I didn't even have to think about it. I had read it every day on my coconut.

"*Interesting.* I-n-t-e-r-e-s-t-i-n-g. *Interesting.*"

"Correct," said Mr. Allen. "Ladies and gentlemen, our new spelling bee champion."

He grabbed my arm and held it above my head like I had just won a boxing match against Oscar de la Hoya. The overflowing bleachers gave me a standing ovation, and the back of my neck tickled.

Mom, Dad, Uncle Max, and the manny congratulated me while the kids filed back toward their classrooms for the rest of the school day. A man from the newspaper took my picture and interviewed me for next Wednesday's paper.

Mom asked what I'd like for dinner that night, and then she and Dad left. They had to go back to work. The manny and Uncle Max walked me back to my classroom. The manny didn't walk. He did cartwheels, but he stopped when he heard Mr. Allen coming around the corner. We laughed after Mr. Allen had passed us because the manny had said, "Hello, sir," like he hadn't been doing anything unusual.

Uncle Max said good-bye, and the manny gave me a high five. I could still hear them laughing as I went into my classroom, until my class started cheering for me when I walked through the door. Mrs. House and the kids had a party for me, complete with cake and punch. The kids in my class excitedly told their version of the spelling bee.

"I got so nervous when the chair flew out from underneath you. I thought for sure you were too jittery to spell," said Sarah.

"I knew you were going to win the whole time," said Scotty.

Craig didn't say anything. He just sat at his

desk and ate cake while the other kids swarmed around me like bees.

At recess that afternoon I saw Craig walk over behind the Dumpster. I jumped down from the monkey bars and followed him because I thought that he might be writing something mean next to my name.

When I got there, Craig was crying.

He saw that I was standing there, and yelled at me.

"Get out of here, spelling nerd. If you tell anyone, I'll smack you."

He put his face right into mine and pushed his chin out as a threat.

I reached into my front pocket and pulled out a Sharpie. I always carry a Sharpie because you never know when you might need one.

"Here. If you want to sign your name on the Dumpster." I smiled at him. He took the pen, and I said, "Okay. Bye."

I ran back over to join Sarah, Scotty, and my other friends on top of the monkey bars. I didn't tell any of them that I had seen Craig crying behind the Dumpster. Not even Sarah.

Craig didn't say a word to me the rest of the day.

After school, on my way to the bus, I stopped by the Dumpster to see if Craig had written anything by my name. He had. Written right next to KEATS DALINGER was CRAIG PRICE.

I got on the bus.

"Congratulations on the spellin' bee, darlin'," said the bus driver.

Darlin'. D-a-r-l-i-n-apostrophe. *Darlin'.*

September 28

I won the all-school spelling bee. I heard Mrs. House talking to one of the other teachers in the hallway about me, but she didn't know I was listening. She said that this was the first time a student from her classroom had won. India walked by them, and Mrs. House said, "Are you proud of your brother?" Mrs. House turned to the other teacher and said, "That's Keats's big sister."

I saw Craig crying in my secret spot. He didn't tell me what he was crying about. The manny said that he might have been crying because he wished he had won the spelling bee. Or maybe he had had a fight with his mother. Or his dog died. He said people cry for all sorts of reasons. Sometimes you just can't hold it in anymore.

Born on this day: Brigitte Bardot, Ed Sullivan, Hilary Duff

34 Let's Get Out of Here, Scoob

For Halloween this year I wanted to be something spectacular. *Spectacular* is another word that Sarah likes to use with magical hand motions. She usually says it when I ask her about her vacations.

"How was your trip to Venice?"

"Spectacular. They have the most unbelievable pigeons there."

"How was your visit to your cousins' house in Wisconsin?"

"Spectacular. There weren't any mosquitoes."

"How was the airplane ride?"

"Dreadful."

She likes the word *dreadful,* too.

This Halloween, Sarah dressed up as the Eiffel Tower. She and her mom went to Paris for summer vacation and to visit Sarah's mom's college roommate. Sarah's been talking about the Eiffel Tower ever since. She says that the lights on it at night are spectacular. She built a miniature Eiffel

Tower out of cardboard and white Christmas lights. She wore it so that she was inside the tower and all you could see were her legs and her arms hanging out. She said that I should go as the Leaning Tower of Pisa, but I didn't want to walk around leaning sideways all night.

Instead I dressed up as Scooby Doo. He's my favorite cartoon character, as you might remember from the underwear incident. I learned what an incident was last year from Ms. Grant. We had to draw a poster for National Dental Month. I took my poster board home, and India drew a picture of a tooth sitting in a dentist's chair with a gas mask on. She wrote the words A BRUSH WITH SUCCESS at the top. I colored it.

My poster won the contest, and they hung it in Dr. Craighead's dentist office.

A few weeks later Ms. Grant needed somebody to draw posters for the school carnival. She said that I had done such a beautiful job on my dental poster that she wanted me to do these posters for her. I asked if I could do them at home, but she said she needed them quickly and handed me some poster board. I drew three posters, and each one was worse than the last. When I turned them in, she knew that I hadn't done my own dental poster. All that these new posters had on them were stick people holding balloons.

I told her that India had drawn my poster and I had colored it. I explained that Andy Warhol's entire career as an artist was based on that same philosophy. Uncle Max had been reading *The Philosophy of Andy Warhol*, and we had talked about it at dinner.

She called my mom about the "incident."

Housman growled at me when I wore my Scooby Doo costume. He acted like he was going to attack my ankle, but instead he ran to my room and hid under my bed.

The manny dressed up as Shaggy, Scooby Doo's best friend. He said things like "Zoinks" and "Let's get out of here, Scoob."

I said things back like "Ruh-roh" and "Scooby Dooby Doo" in my best Scooby impersonation, which wasn't very good.

Uncle Max put on a white sweater and a red scarf and went as Fred. Lulu put on her miniskirt and a red wig and went as Daphne.

She loved being the pretty one.

India loved being the smart one. She put on an orange turtleneck and dark-framed glasses and went as Velma, the intellectual one who always loses her glasses.

Belly dressed up as Scrappy Doo, the smaller, tougher version of Scooby Doo.

The day of the school Halloween parade the manny walked with my class. I asked Mrs. House if he could walk with me because he was my sidekick. Like Batman and Robin. The Lone Ranger and Tonto. Siegfried and Roy.

Mrs. House said it would be fine.

I don't think she had heard the fiasco story from last year's Halloween parade. She was dressed up as Scarlett O'Hara, with a big hoopskirt. I made sure not to walk anywhere near her.

Ms. Grant remembered. She was dressed up as a cowgirl, with chaps and spurs. She even had a lariat. When she saw me, she smiled, but I could tell she was thinking about how our entire class fell on her last year. She looked like she wanted to lasso me and tie me up like they do the calves at the rodeo.

Two summers ago Dad took us to a rodeo that came to town with the fair. I wore cowboy boots and accidentally stepped in horse poop. I didn't cry because that's what cowboy boots are for, and it made me feel like a real cowboy. I did cry when they did the calf roping. They roped a calf around the neck from the top of a horse and then ran over and tied it up as fast as they could. When they were done, they put their hands up in victory like they had just wrestled an elephant instead of a forty-pound calf. It looked mean. I told Dad I didn't like small things being picked on by bigger ones. We left early to get cotton candy and ride the Ferris wheel.

The manny and I threw Scooby snacks to the people watching the parade. They were really little bags of candy corn, but we called them Scooby snacks.

Craig was dressed in the same costume he wore last year. It wasn't much of a costume. He wore a ripped-up white T-shirt and ripped-up jeans that had red dye all over them that looked like blood. He had a fake hatchet attached to the top of his head, with bloodred makeup around it and dripping down his face.

He walked with the manny and me during the parade.

He said that he liked our costumes.

The manny gave him Scooby snacks to throw.

He shoved most of them into his own pocket.

That night the manny and Uncle Max took us trick-or-treating in the Volkswagen Eurovan. We made cardboard panels for the side of the Eurovan that said THE MYSTERY MACHINE.

We went up to each house as a group. Most people laughed when they saw our costumes. Especially when Belly would call them a wise guy and demand miniature Milky Ways or pop-corn balls.

One man gave us extra candy.

One older lady didn't know who we were supposed to be. She looked at Lulu and said, "Oh my, you must be Britney Spears and her backup singers."

She gave us Smarties.

She reminded me of Grandma.

We trick-or-treated at Craig's house. Craig's mom answered the door, while his dad sat on the couch and watched television. His mom yelled to his dad that he had to see our costumes.

He said, "I can't. I'm watching the *bleep-bleep* game right now."

Only he didn't say "*bleep-bleep*." He said the word that I heard Dad say the time he smashed his finger with a hammer. The same word they bleep out on television, but you can still tell what they're saying.

Craig's mom looked at us with a fake smile and said, "It's just the way men are, huh?"

On the way back to the car the manny grabbed Uncle Max's plastic pumpkin from his hand and yelled, "I'm stealing all of your Now and Laters."

Uncle Max tackled him and held him down, pretending he was going to let spit fall on the manny's face. He spit out a little bit and then sucked it back up. Spit out a little more and sucked it back up. Uncle Max has done this to me before, but I hit my meltdown limit, which usually gets me a trip to the ice cream store. The manny didn't hit his meltdown limit. He started laughing and gave the pumpkin back.

Lulu hates spit. She told them that they were immature.

In the car the manny stuck his tongue out at Uncle Max and went, "Nyaaa."

There was a yellow Now and Later on the end of his tongue.

I think Craig's mom is wrong about the way men are.

When we got home, Lulu, India, and I dumped our candy-filled plastic pumpkins all over the living-room floor. I began sorting my loot to see what I had gotten. I made a pile of Bottle Caps candy for the manny. They're his favorite.

Belly was already asleep, with a green Dum Dum sucker stuck to the side of her face.

Dad came in and tried to steal a Pixy Stix from India, but we caught him and screamed for Mom.

He said, "I would've gotten away with it too, if it hadn't been for you meddling kids."

October 31

Halloween

I got so much candy for Halloween this year. People give you more candy if they don't have to ask what you're supposed to be. Mrs. Dean was handing out cotton candy.

We went trick-or-treating at Craig's house. It smelled like the bowling alley. Like cigarettes and feet. Craig's dad is grumpy. He cussed at Craig's mom in front of us, but it didn't seem to bother her. Poor Craig. I have Dad, Uncle Max, and the manny, and Craig just has a bleeping dad who can't even stop watching television to look at Halloween costumes. I bet that's why he cries behind the Dumpster.

Born on this day: Helmut Newton, Dan Rather, John Keats

35 No Wedgies on Thanksgiving

My Halloween candy is always gone by November 3. Lulu still has her Halloween candy at Valentine's Day. She keeps it on the top shelf of her closet, where Belly can't reach it. I can reach it if the manny holds me up. We did that only once. Lulu caught us and made us pay her for the candy we had taken. A quarter for my bubble gum. A dollar for the manny's Now and Later.

She charged him more because she said he should know better.

I try to save my candy, but I just can't. The manny had to sit down with me and tell me what gluttony was. He told me that it was when something was done excessively, like eating too much or buying more than you need.

I said, "You mean like you are with cashmere socks?"

He messed up the back of my hair and said, "Have another candy bar, turkey."

He had been calling us turkeys the entire month of November because it was almost Thanksgiving. He and Uncle Max came over to have Thanksgiving dinner with us. Uncle Max made the turkey. Mom and Dad made everything else.

Cranberry sauce. Sweet potatoes. Pumpkin pie.

The manny and I were in charge of setting and decorating the table. The manny doesn't like to cook for himself. He likes to eat out at restaurants. He told me once that he uses his oven like a closet and keeps his sweaters in it.

I think he was joking, but I'll look if I ever go over to his house.

I made name cards to place at each person's chair at the dinner table so that they would know where to sit. I wrote their names in the fancy bubble letters that India showed me how to do. I wrote TURKEY on the manny's name card instead of his name.

I put myself between the manny and Uncle Max.

Mom was next to Uncle Max. Then Belly. Lulu. Dad. India. The manny.

Lulu and India baked a pecan pie. Grandma taught them how a few years ago when they had a girls' night sleepover at Grandma's house. I got to stay home with Dad. We ate chips and salsa and watched *Star Wars*. I drank three root beers and had a nightmare that night. Dad said I was screaming, "I love you, Chewbacca."

India wore a Christmas apron that was red and green striped. Lulu wore Grandma's old apron that said KISS THE COOK on it. Every time Uncle Max read it, he kissed Lulu on the forehead.

She finally traded aprons with India.

Dad made mashed potatoes. Mom made stuffing. Uncle Max kept checking his turkey.

Belly sat on the floor of the kitchen and ate gravy out of a little bowl. She scooped up the gravy with her shoehorn that she had gotten at the shoe store. She thinks it's a spoon. Housman sat next to her, waiting for her to drop some on the floor.

The manny and I chose a gold-colored tablecloth and matching napkins for the table. We put white candles down the center of the table and lit them. Around the candles we spread pinecones from the tree in our yard. As a finishing touch I taped the turkeys that we had made the day before on the backs of the chairs.

We had made the turkeys by outlining our hands on construction paper and then putting tails and beaks on them. You could tell which turkey Lulu had made because it was huge. I showed her how much bigger hers was than the rest, and she chased me and gave me a wedgie.

"No wedgies on Thanksgiving," said the manny. "Save them for Christmas."

Uncle Max thought the table was beautiful. He laughed and gave me a high five when he saw the manny's name card said TURKEY. He put the carved turkey on the counter next to the table, and Mom put bowls of potatoes, stuffing, and green beans out. We served our own plates like we were in a cafeteria.

The manny piled turkey, sweet potatoes, mashed potatoes and gravy, stuffing, and green beans on his plate. When I saw how much food the manny had on his plate, I reminded him about the word *gluttony*.

He put back two green beans.

I put all of the same stuff on my plate that the manny put on his.

After we stacked our plates with food, we sat at the table. Belly sat in her booster seat.

It's a tradition at our house to give thanks before we eat. We go around the table and take turns saying what we're thankful for. Last year I buckled under the pressure. I stood up and said that I was thankful for the John Denver and the Muppets Christmas album. I knew it sounded silly, but I *was* thankful for it. We had been listening to it that morning and I was still singing

"It's in Every One of Us" in my head.

It's my favorite song.

I felt better when Belly said she was thankful for rocks.

This Thanksgiving I got to give thanks first.

I stood up and said, "I'm thankful that everybody I know is interesting."

I had decided I was going to say that two days ago when I was looking at the BE INTERESTING coconut on my dresser.

The manny stood up and said that he was thankful for cashmere socks, red wine, and all the new additions to his family.

I think he was talking about us.

India stood up and said, "I'm thankful that Grandma lived with us this summer."

Her face got really red when she said this, and she sat down really fast, before she started to cry.

Dad put his hand on India's shoulder and stood up.

He said, "I'm thankful that I have four wonderful children and a brilliant wife to come home to every night."

The back of my neck tickled like it does when I hear the word *divine*.

When Lulu stood up, she spoke like she was receiving an award.

"I want to take this time to say that I'm

thankful that I made the principal's honor roll again this quarter. I'm also thankful for Fletcher."

Everybody at the table went, "Wooooo."

Some kids in my class did that last year when Sarah and I were swinging side by side on the swings on the playground, and I yelled, "Look, Sarah, we're married."

Belly stood up and gave thanks for Housman and for DecapiTina, who had gravy all over her headless body. Housman carried DecapiTina around in his mouth for two days after Thanksgiving.

When Mom stood up, she had watery eyes like she gets when she walks through the perfume section of the department store in the mall.

She said, "I'm thankful that my family is here together and that Grandma is dancing outside in the garden."

I looked out to the garden and smiled at Grandma.

Uncle Max was the last one to stand up to say what he was thankful for. He lifted his glass and thanked Mom and Dad for hosting Thanksgiving.

He said, "I'm thankful for many things this year, especially for my family."

When he said this, he moved his glass in a circle in front of him.

Then he cleared his throat and said some

more. "I'm most thankful this year that Matthew has come into my life."

My ears wiggled. Who was Matthew? I looked around to see if anybody else was confused. Then I saw that Uncle Max was looking at the manny.

Uncle Max put his hand on my shoulder and leaned over me toward the manny, so that I was in between their chests.

The back of my neck tickled.

Lulu squealed.

She hates it when people kiss.

November 22

FANTASTICAL!!!!

Birthday Biographies

May 11

Martha Graham—American dancer and choreographer whose legacy is credited as inspiration for modern dance troupes.

Salvador Dalí—Spanish surrealist painter.

Irving Berlin—A musician and composer who wrote many recognizable songs, such as "White Christmas" and "God Bless America."

May 16

Liberace—Piano player known for his flashy way of dress as well as for his music.

Olga Korbut—Female gymnast best known for competing in the 1972 Summer Olympics.

Christian Lacroix—French haute couture clothing designer.

May 22

Sir Laurence Olivier—Award-winning actor who received an Oscar for his performance as Hamlet.

Mary Cassatt—American-born impressionist painter.

Harvey Milk—First openly gay person to be elected to San

Francisco's city council. He was murdered by a former city supervisor in City Hall along with San Francisco mayor George Moscone.

May 26

Dr. Sally Ride—The first American woman in space, in 1983.

Stevie Nicks—Singer who fronts the band Fleetwood Mac.

John Wayne—American actor known for his Western movies of the 1950s. He won an Oscar for his role in *True Grit* in 1969.

May 29

John F. Kennedy—Thirty-fifth president of the United States, famous for his speech that included "Ask not what your country can do for you—ask what you can do for your country." Killed by an assassin's bullet on November 22, 1963.

Bob Hope—Hollywood entertainer known around the world for performing for United States troops that were stationed overseas. Considered an American icon.

T. H. White—Author of *The Sword in the Stone*. He was a novelist as well as a poet.

June 1

Keats Dalinger—The narrator of this book, he was named in honor of John Keats and is an all-around *interesting* guy. Builder of award-winning LEGO creations.

June 27

Helen Keller—A deaf and blind woman who overcame her

obstacles to become a writer, a teacher, and an inspiration to those with disabilities as well as to those without.

Ross Perot—Founder of Electronic Data Systems, who ran in the 1992 and 1996 presidential elections.

Captain Kangaroo—Much-loved host of his own children's television show. His real name was Bob Keeshan.

June 28

John Elway—Former member of the National Football League's Denver Broncos. He was named Most Valuable Player of Super Bowl XXXIII.

Henry VIII—King of England (1509–47) who used his power for his own benefit and was often morally questioned. He was married six times and is known for having his wives executed.

Gilda Radner—Comedian and actress who was in the original cast of *Saturday Night Live*. She founded Gilda's Club, an organization that lends support to those living with cancer as well as to their families. She died of cancer in 1989. Gilda's Club is still an active organization.

July 6

Frida Kahlo—Mexican painter who used her marital and emotional problems in her work. She was married to fellow Mexican painter Diego Rivera.

Janet Leigh—Film actress known for her role in *Psycho*; mother to actress Jamie Lee Curtis.

Sylvester Stallone—American action star who most notably played the boxer Rocky in the movie *Rocky*.

July 8

John D. Rockefeller—A major figure in the oil industry, he was once thought of as the most successful man in the world.

Philip Johnson—An architect who was as famous for his Glass House as he was for the dark-framed round glasses that he wore. He was the first architecture director for the Museum of Modern Art.

Kevin Bacon—American actor who appeared in *Footloose* and *Apollo 13* as well as more than fifty other motion pictures.

July 9

David Hockney—British painter whose works include his famed pool series and photo collages.

Barbara Cartland—Twentieth-century British romance novelist.

Tom Hanks—Two-time Oscar-winning actor who appeared in *Forrest Gump* and *Apollo 13*.

July 22

Alex Trebek—Host of the television game show *Jeopardy*.

Rose Kennedy—Mother of nine children, including President John F. Kennedy and two former senators, Robert Kennedy and Edward Kennedy.

Oscar de la Renta—High-end fashion designer who created an empire with clothes, fragrances, and home apparel. He is originally from the Dominican Republic but now resides in New York City, where he sits on the board of several foundations, including UNICEF.

August 11

Hulk Hogan—Wrestler with the World Wrestling Entertainment and then World Championship Wrestling who later went on to become a movie actor.

Alex Haley—Author of the novel *Roots*, which traces his ancestry through six generations from Africa to America.

Jerry Falwell—Baptist preacher who is known for his political activism. His controversial views propagate nonacceptance of the differences in people, including sexuality.

August 19

Malcolm Forbes—American publisher who took over his father's magazine, *Forbes*, which caters to and lists top businessmen.

Bill Clinton—The forty-second president of the United States. He was raised in Arkansas and overcame an underprivileged childhood.

Coco Chanel—Paris fashion designer who specialized in elegant casual wear, such as women's slacks and suits.

September 1

Rocky Marciano—Former shoe worker who became the heavyweight boxing champion of the world in 1952.

Lily Tomlin—Actress and comedian who appeared in *The Incredible Shrinking Woman* and many other movies.

Gloria Estefan—Latina singer who sang lead for the Miami Sound Machine.

September 3

Memphis Slim—Jazz and blues singer and pianist.

Alan Ladd—American actor who appeared in such films as *The Carpetbaggers*, *Citizen Kane*, and *Shane*.

Marguerite Higgins—A news reporter who became the first woman to win the Pulitzer for international reporting.

September 4

Beyoncé Knowles—Pop recording artist who releases solo albums as well as albums with the group Destiny's Child.

Paul Harvey—Radio personality known for a segment called "The Rest of the Story." Inducted into the Radio Hall of Fame in 1990.

Daniel Burnham—Architect who designed the recognizable Flatiron Building in New York City.

September 7

Grandma Moses—American folk artist whose real name was Anna Mary Robertson Moses.

Queen Elizabeth I—Daughter of Henry VIII and Anne Boleyn. She reigned as queen of England for forty-five years but never married or had children.

Buddy Holly—A rock-and-roll legend from the 1950s. At the height of his popularity he was killed in a plane crash along with Ritchie Valens and the Big Bopper in 1959.

September 8

Patsy Cline—Country singer from the 1950s and 1960s who opened doors for future female singers. She was killed in a plane crash in 1963. She was thirty years old.

Peter Sellers—Comic actor best known as Inspector Clouseau from the Pink Panther movies.

Pink—Born Alecia Moore. A singer popular for both her music and her ever-changing hairstyles.

September 19

Dr. Amy Whittington—Naturopathic doctor. Sister to the author of this book and mother to the author's nephew, Fletcher Christian Whittington.

Sir William Golding—British novelist who wrote *The Lord of the Flies*.

Adam West—Actor who played Batman in the 1960s television series.

September 20

Sister Kenny—A nurse who worked in the fight against polio.

Ferdinand "Jelly Roll" Morton—a jazz and piano player who formed a band called the Red Hot Peppers.

Dr. Joyce Brothers—Began career by winning $64,000 on the game show *$64,000 Question*. Currently writes daily newspaper column on psychology.

September 28

Brigitte Bardot—French actress known for her beauty and acting as well as the famous men she dated and married

Ed Sullivan—Host of the *Ed Sullivan Show*, which ran on Sunday nights for more than twenty years and had such guests as Elvis Presley and the Beatles.

Hilary Duff—Actress and singer who starred in the television series *Lizzie McGuire* as well as the movie *A Cinderella Story*.

October 31

Helmut Newton—A visual artist whose photographs have been in fashion magazines such as *Elle* and *Vogue*.

Dan Rather—A former White House correspondent who was the anchor for *CBS Evening News*.

John Keats—An English poet whose work is both sensual and philosophical. He lived a tragic life, which ended at the age of twenty-five from tuberculosis.